The Raven of Craven

By Loy Seattle Phillips

Artwork by S. Lindor: Lindorcreations@yahoo.co.uk

Loy Seattle Phillips: loydinium@gmail.com

A special thank you to the following for their contributions:

Dr Rebecca J Harrison
Suzette Lindor
Marva Gregorio De Souza

Dedicated to Katherine

Table of Contents

Water

Full moon, white
New moon, black
Come home to me
Heal my wound
The Earth, sun and moon align
In my orbit, water rides the tide
When the law of gravity beckons, she must obey
What water reveals when it recedes, I'm here to say

-Adleme

The Black Jacobins

All is black.

Nothing is visible in the darkness until a match is struck. Flickers of gold catch the tiny explosion of light. The flame is brought to a wick, which quickly burns down to meet a bone coloured candle.

By holding the candle up to his line of vision the contents of the vault comes into clear view. Though low in volume, his whisper echoes throughout the arched tiles. His French perfectly marries Haitian Patois and a Parisian dialect, "Look. Look at all of this gold. I didn't realise there would be so much. There must be thousands in here."

Another voice responds in a similar decibel and dialect, "Sukhbir said four hundred thousand bars and all of it stolen from Africa. The sight of it is both beautiful and sickening."

The two men stand awestruck as they examine the countless rows of gold bullion running the length of the vault, stacked uniformly like coffins of fallen soldiers.

The man holding the candle picks up one of the shiny bricks, "How many times has this been refined to purge it of our blood?"

He then holds the light to his colleague as he awaits a response to his hypothetical question. His friend is a tall statuesque man of the darkest of hues and spectacularly angled features, "My brother, we haven't the time to ponder such issues. We must make haste."

The man holding the candle is himself a tall, square shouldered black man, though of a warm cinnamon brown complexion, almond shaped eyes, with a distinctive widow's peak punctuating his forehead. In compliance with his friend's wishes, he nods and stuffs the gold bar into a saddle bag slung across his torso. As does his companion, "We must go."

Through a round hole in the floor, they drop down to the sewer below. Their black leather boots splash into ankle deep murky water. They return a grate to a round hole in what was the floor but from their present perspective of the tunnel, is a curved red brick ceiling. The flame of the candle is slowly and carefully brought closer to two sticks of brown dynamite wedged into holes in the grate cut out for handles.

Whimsically, the candle bearer asks his friend, "Do you think they'll notice we were here?"

"Not only will they know we were here, they will know that we are not content to sneak away like scared little mice with crumbs from master's table." His high cheekbones are further accentuated by his broad smile.

The flame is brought closer yet to a long and coiled wick until it finally it makes contact creating a burst of white light. "Run!" The candle bearer drops their only source of light as they tear through the shallow water.

They run through a labyrinth of tunnels and at each turn snatch tiny scraps of red rags from nails, which have been carefully placed to fall out of the mortar when pulled on. Though shallow, the water conspires against them causing the occasional stumble.

"Look there." the men feast their eyes on a ladder just beyond the last scrap of red fabric.

"Wait, what happened to the..."

An explosion shakes the ground beneath their feet causing them to fall against the curved walls of the sewer. The ceiling rains rubble onto them. By the time the two men stagger to their feet, the tunnel is full of smoke and soot, further reducing their visibility in the darkness and impeding their ability to breath - they cough violently and clutch their ears.

With greater fortune than Hansel and Gretel, they stagger on to the last of their bread crumbs. The darker of the two men pulls the last red rag off the nail and kisses it before tucking it into his pocket.

They make their way up the ladder.

Above ground, an elderly black man with a white woolly afro and dressed in tattered clothes stands on a corner just beyond the steel manhole cover, where little streams of smoke waft out. But it is the giant plumes of smoke billowing over St Paul's Cathedral that has his attention. He tries to conceal the glint in his cataract covered eye.

A group of finely dressed Englishmen in top hat and tails run past the old man and the manhole cover, which bangs below their feet. They are oblivious to what lays beneath them. The elderly black man tilts his hat to them but they are oblivious to him too. Instead, they focus on joining other pedestrians as they rush towards the junction of the Bank of England and the Royal Exchange, where a crowd gathers around the epicentre of the underground explosion.

Once the Englishmen have created a sufficient distance between themselves and the manhole cover, the elderly black man grabs a broom propped up under a street sign for Ludgate Hill. After a quick look over both shoulders, he turns the broom upside down and uses the handle to levy the manhole cover open.

The two men pop up. They're covered in dust, still coughing and struggling to breathe but manage to give the elder of them a surreptitious handshake before calmly walking in the opposite direction of St Paul's. With each step, they brush their breaches clean.

The elderly black man smiles as he slides the cover closed. Despite his feeble appearance, he swiftly swings his broom back around and sweeps a combination of mud, horse manure, and straw over the manhole cover.

Mi Nuh Sen You Nuh Come

All is white.

Swirling around chimney stacks and black outlines of naked tree branches, a snow flurry picks up speed. Below, black rails mark the borders of giant white houses on Westbourne Terrace. Rows and rows of houses align in battalion like perfection.

A slight rut separates the pavement from Praed Street, where the snow has turned into a mixture of greys and browns. This earthy palette dissipates, turning whiter further down the road past Gloucester Terrace, Brook Mews North and then on to Craven Hill, where the snow is whitest of all.

A few bundled figures dash around attempting to evade the snow as if it were burning their skin. But not her. Christian Waters sails down the street impervious to the elements. The snow whirls around her too but seems to melt before touching her long black hooded cape.

Christian runs her hands along an unpainted iron rail in front of a house whose shell is only roughly completed. Banging and tinkering of all sorts echo out from the cavernous innards. The spikes on the railings are sharp and their swirly details run deep under her fingers as she traces the line of the spear upward and then along the connecting rail until they merge into a freshly painted railing. The black paint is barely visible on her black leather glove.

She looks up to find a set of unfinished oak doors guarded by four Ionic columns. The doors look naked absent of any paint or hardware. Instead, a leaf of paper with "No. 7" is tacked to the left door. Much like Christian, the inclement weather fails to take effect on the house. It stands tall and strong.

Approaching from the opposite direction, two women scurry as fast as their corseted waists and hoop skirts will allow. Though not readily visible, it quickly becomes apparent that one of the women is cradling a blanketed baby and the other a small white dog. The voices of the women become increasingly audible as they approach.

Christian takes a few steps back until she is standing in front of the neighbouring property of 6 Craven Hill Gardens, the home of the unpainted rail. By lowering her head, she is able to hide her face from view under her black bonnet, leaving just the white frill from the lining visible. She then cranes her head ever so slightly to train her hearing in the direction of the approaching voices but it is difficult to discern their words over the crying infant.

The two women ascend the steps and proceed to the raw oak doors of 7 Craven Hill Gardens.

"This has gone on long enough. Since your father will not speak to Mr Fen about these doors, then I will."

Mrs Claiborne, the older of the two women, pulls on a coarsely twined rope - a rope more likely to be found in a shipping yard - and a faint tinkle of a bell is heard from within the house. "Just look at the state of this place. What must people think..."

Mrs Claiborne leans back on the railing between the Ionic columns, only to receive the same black smudge on her black leather glove. "For the love of... Who paints on a day like this!"

The younger woman, Elouise, continues to console the baby by rocking to and fro as she looks up at the sky. "Don't start on Mr Fen again mother. It's almost April. Who knew the weather would turn like this, neither of us certainly did. This snow came out of nowhere."

Elouise is about to return her focus to her baby when she catches sight of Christian, who is still standing just within view from the porch, her bonnet still shielding her face. Mrs Claiborne follows Elouise's gaze until she too catches sight of the figure in black standing in the white snow. The front door opens but neither women enter. Instead, they remain transfixed on the mysterious figure before them.

Mrs Claiborne speaks first, "I say... can I be of assistance?"

A cowering diminutive young woman clad in a maid's uniform steps out from the house and tentatively seeks out the object of distraction.

Mrs Claiborne begins her descent of the small staircase leading from the porch but freezes midway when Christian shows signs of life. As though she had never stopped walking, Christian strides on boldly. Her white petticoat and long black skirt bustle with each step. As she approaches number 7, she raises her bonnet revealing her bronze coloured skin and apple seed eyes, which are now solely focused on Mrs Claiborne, who is standing in the middle of the three-step staircase.

Christian's dark brown leather grip displays the many years of use well. The embossed initials, *LSW* become more readily visible when the bag is switched from her right hand to the left. Christian's newly freed right hand extends to Mrs Claiborne.

"Good mor...," Christian looks over her shoulder at the sunless sky, her eyes tracing from east to west. "Let's make that good afternoon... Mrs Claiborne." Her hand remains suspended in midair as Mrs Claiborne recoils back up the stairs.

Christian steps closer until she is at the foot of the of the bottom step. Upon approach, Puddles, the Maltese in Mrs Claiborne's arms, growls at Christian. Mrs Claiborne makes no attempt to quell her dog's angst as Christian lowers her unreceived hand.

Despite now standing on the top step, Mrs Claiborne is the same height as Christian. The two lock gazes. Christian continues, "I believe you are expecting me."

Mrs Claiborne shakes her head ever so slightly and mumbles, "I shouldn't think so," which is only audible to Christian.

"I'm Christian Waters, your new governess."

A freshly painted white door swings open, "...and this is your room, mam. I'm just down the hall, so we'll be neighbours." The meek voice of Victoria Tarn matches her frail presence.

Victoria enters the attic room, the contents of the copper pail she carries rattles with her movement. Christian follows her in but has to stoop a little to fit under the door frame.

A single occupancy sized bed with a black wrought iron frame is just beyond the door and tucked into the left corner of the room. Above the head of the bed, a thick black wooden cross. Opposite the bed, a tiny fireplace, and mantel. Set before the fireplace a spoked-back wooden chair and round table permitting space for one. Covering the table, a dark red threadbare tablecloth. Christian's eyes fix on a journal bound in brown paper and laid in the centre of the table. Aside from the journal, there's only enough space for one more item – an oil lamp. While the furnishings give evidence of many previous owners, the crisp white walls mark the stark newly painted room, in the newly built house.

Wedged in the corner, next to the fireplace is a narrow bookcase. Its shelves are speckled with voids indicating where chunks of books have been removed.

Christian makes her way to a small sash window in between the bed and bookcase. On the window ledge, a large blue and white delft bowl and matching jug depicting hastily painted flowers almost obscure the view of the back garden. Snow barely covers the boxed shaped garden – its black soil still pierces the white crust. A little timber shed in the corner bears the only signs of life by way of a set of footprints leading in and out of its door.

To the left of the bowl and jug, Christian discovers a dying African violet. She drops her bag to the floor and picks up the little terracotta pot examining the charred looking leaves. "Oh, I tried my best to keep it alive but...," Victoria tries to explain.

"Too much light, too much water, too much cold," Christian says as she looks over her shoulder to find Victoria cowering in the doorway. Christian tries to soften her criticism with a smile. She relocates the tiny pot to the middle of the tiny table but to accommodate this she has to move the lamp to the bookcase.

"There, that should be the right amount of light. It's out of the draft and will be warmed by my fire. Now, all we have to do is ensure not too much water. Problem solved?"

Victoria nods nervously, "Yes Mam."

Christian unties the black grosgrain ribbon under her chin and removes her bonnet. Her hair appears to be fashioned into a chignon but when Christian unclasps a giant tortoise shell clip, four thick luscious braids fall down her back. Victoria struggles to keep her eyes off the plaits as Christian approaches a set of coat hooks next to the door frame, where she suspends her bonnet and cape.

"Can I fetch you anything mam, surely you must be in need of something after your journey from America?"

Still smiling warmly, "Thank you but I'm fine and please call me Christian."

"Can't mam, forenames ain't permitted with staff. I'm to call you Miss Waters mam."

"Then it will just be between us. In here, it will be Christian and...?"

Victoria steps in from the doorway. What's left of the afternoon light catches her freckled nose, blue eyes and tufts of blonde hair peeking out from under her white cap. "It's Victoria mam. Victoria Tarn."

Christian extends her hand to Victoria, who tentatively mimics the gesture but doesn't quite meet her halfway. Consequently, Christian has to step into the handshake and pump but Victoria's arm is utterly flaccid.

"You call that a handshake!" Victoria covers her mouth as she giggles. Christian extends her hand once more, "Again!"

A bit more assuredly, Victoria takes Christian's hand and tries to reciprocate the pump. "Well, it was nice to meet Miss Tarn but it's even better to meet Victoria."

"Thank you, Christian."

"If there's nothing else I would like a little nap before I meet the girls."

"No m... Christian, there's nothing else."

Christian shakes out the folded bed linens left at the bottom of the bed and begins to tuck it in under the striped mattress. Victoria attempts to assist but her effort is rebuffed by Christian, "Thank you Victoria but I can manage."

Instead, Victoria removes several lumps of coal from her copper pail as she makes her way to the fireplace. "Just to say, we wasn't expecting you so soon. I almost got your room ready but not the fireplace. I don't normally light the fires until later in the day, but I can light yours now if you'd like."

"I'm fine, as is. But thank you Victoria."

"And that there's a washroom just down the hall past Mrs Farraige's room, she's the cook. And there's an indoor privy right next to it!"

"Ah, good to know."

"I've never had an indoor privy 'til I came here to live." Victoria's comment does not seem to register with Christian who continues making her bed. "I best get on with my chores."

"Yes, please don't let me take up any more of your time. Though, I would love the opportunity to get to know you... but that will come in due course."

"Yes ma... Christian."

Victoria backs out of the room and closes the door. Her smile reveals tiny teeth like those found in a child's mouth.

"What do you mean it doesn't matter? Have you completely lost your mind!"

The oak panelled walls and doors to Claiborne's study have little to no effect on the raised voices coming from within. As Mrs Claiborne raises her voice, so do the yaps coming from her dog. Every syllable rings out through the house and possibly yonder. All that hear, be it in the house or passersby, pretend that they can't.

"Ivy, you saw the same references as I and you were quite pleased to learn her father was a well-traveled Englishman. 'Oh, how lovely, a daughter of an English Quaker' I believe were your exact words. Pleased as punch to bring an American, a foreigner, into our home then but now that you know she's... she's..."

"... a nigger! Ha! Should have known you can't bring yourself to say it."

"Now, just you wait a minute. I'll not tolerate that talk in this house."

"Why? If we're to have a nigger in our house, then we're to say we've a nigger in our house."

Claiborne's cognac coloured high-back Chester chair squeaks in relief as he rises from it. His immense presence eclipses the painting of his younger self, in a crisp red riding jacket, jodhpurs, and shiny top hat. His stormy North Sea blue eyes are now barely visible under his prominent bushy brow. What's left of his wavy black locks are grey and fuzzy. His nostrils flare as though he were literally breathing fire through them. "Listen to me Ivy and listen to me good. You will never refer to her in that manner again or so help me god..."

"Don't you threaten me. The time for you to assert yourself as the man of this house has come and gone. You had the opportunity to keep us in our family seat. *My* family seat. And you couldn't even manage that. Now you're in no position to lecture me on what I can and cannot say! All you had to do is listen to Uncle Albert and we would have been making a fortune is instead of worrying about every penny."

"Not this old pony again. I'm a farmer Ivy. As was my father before me and before him and so on, for as far back as I can trace. I'm tired of telling you that I know nothing of machines and factories that churn out imitation Derby. Nor do I want to. And as for your Uncle Albert, well he isn't your Uncle for starters. He is the half-brother to your father's second wife. If my memory serves me correctly you didn't even want to know him until he came into money. He's not so low born now, is he Ivy? You can't wait to fall on bended knee for your dear old Uncle Albert. Ha! If you'd seen him sloshing about in the mud, hauling clay..."

"You're one to talk about sloshing about in the mud. Look at us. How low we have fallen. *We're* just one notch up from the gypsies in the piggeries and potteries."

"Please woman, clearly you haven't any idea of the gypsies because dare I say, they're a far happier bunch than we." Claiborne falls back into his chair. The leather squeaks again but this time in agony.

"Sir, may I remind you that my family held the Weymouth Estate for five generations until you came along, and you dare talk to me about happiness."

"For the last and final time, your family benefited from five generations of uninterrupted plantation revenue. Was it my fault that abolition came during our day? Let us be grateful for the reparations from His Majesty's Government and the little proceeds I rescued from the sale of Weymouth."

"Grateful?"

Mrs Claiborne rises from her chair. Though standing, she is still only an inch or two taller than her husband, who remains seated. The centre part of her hair is a brilliant white but gradually gives way to a sandy brown chignon. By swinging the door in the study open she reveals a large historic painting in a gilded oak leaf frame hanging in the hallway. It is of a hunting party covering a vast tract of land and in the not too distant background, a manor house of scale and grandeur that could rival the best in England.

"Am I really to be grateful to go from this..." Mrs Claiborne gestures to present surroundings, "...to this Mr George Claiborne?"

"Yes Mrs Claiborne, we ought to be grateful after your reckless spending almost landed us in the poor house. How could I have invested a penny with dear old Uncle Albert with you pissing it away at every opportunity! "

Claiborne, who has now joined his wife in the hall, grabs her arm and snatches Puddles by the scruff of his neck, then slides him down the freshly buffed hall tiles. He drags his wife back into the study and slams the door shut, "It may not be Weymouth but it's home sweet home my darling and you'd do well to make that adjustment."

With Mrs Claiborne still in his grasp, he throws her into the chair. Puddles whimpers outside the door. Claiborne collapses into his high-back, panting as if he'd just run for miles. From a decanter, he pours two shots of whiskey into finely etched glasses. He takes one and gestures for Mrs Claiborne to take the other. She does not.

Without flinching or even blinking, "She's not staying."

Claiborne gulps down his shot of whiskey, "Yes. She. Is."

"I will not be humiliated any further by our downward spiral."

"What is this humiliation you speak of?" Claiborne gulps down the other shot intended for his wife. "There are plenty of great houses with black servants. Why, even the Queen has out and out adopted an African girl and there's plenty more in her employ."

"As a governess? I should think not. Who in their right mind would employ a..." Claiborne fires a warning shot with his yellow stained eyes. Mrs Claiborne makes the adjustment and continues, "... a black woman to educate their children."

"You've read her qualifications Ivy. She's a damn sight more educated than you. So, what the hell do you know about her suitability."

Mrs Claiborne rises to her feet, like a column piercing the earth's crust.

Claiborne pours himself yet another shot and gulps it down just as fast as the first two. "It's a new day Ivy and all I ask is that you give her a chance. We've managed to secure a governess who comes with superior references, a university education, knowledge of a world beyond our borders and, *and* is satisfied with the meagre salary we're offering. Can you not see how very fortunate we are? Who knows, *we* might even be the toast of Bayswater!"

Mrs Claiborne shouts, "Ha! More like Backwater."

"This neighbourhood has already started to attract the most forward thinkers of our day. This little *backwater* may surprise you yet Ivy."

Claiborne rises once more, to the relief of his chair. "Come on, old girl. Let's give it a go." His hand is so large that it engulfs her shoulder, as he places it on her. "I bet she's a bonny lass, yet..." Claiborne looks longingly toward the painting opposite his desk, next to the front door, "I can hardly wait to see her."

Mrs Claiborne's woeful face turns to stone when she realises her husband's melancholy over the painting behind her. She brushes his hand off her shoulder and turns to exit. Puddles, still whimpering away, leaps into her arms the second she opens the door. "Sir, I may have to stomach her wretched presence in this house but I am far from embracing it. You, on the other hand, are far better at it. Always have been and I see, always will be."

"Ivy!"

Mrs Claiborne slams the door shut without looking behind her.

Christian steps back into her room and gently closes the door. She smiles wryly.

※

Victoria hobbles as fast as her sparrow-like legs will carry her down the narrow back staircase to the kitchen. "Mrs Farraige, Mrs Farrraige..."

"Calm down child. I heard every word, same as you. With all that commotion, it was harder not to!"

"No, not that."

Mrs Farraige, stops rubbing a skinned cow's head with large granules of salt but her hands remain firmly on either side of its jaw, as she turns to address Victoria, "So you've seen her, have you?"

Victoria beams with a new found confidence, "I have yes, Mrs Farraige."

"Well child, out with it or do you want to end up on my butcher's block."

"She's ever so tall. And Mrs Farraige, she's dark the likes of which, I ain't never seen before."

"Come now, you mean to say that you never crossed path with one of them darkies in Whitechapel?"

"Yes...but I ain't never spoke to one."

Rolling her eyes, Mrs Farraige returns to rubbing salt into the animal's head. Victoria attempts to regain her attention, "That's not to say she don't seem like a fine person." Mrs Farraige reaches for sprigs of dried rosemary hanging upside down on the wall behind her and proceeds to massage them into the decapitated head along with the salt. "Miss Waters is her name but she said I'm to call her Christian and she's to call me Victoria... but only when we're alone."

Victoria finally succeeds in securing Mrs Farraige's full attention, as she looks up from the glazed eyes staring out aimlessly from the cow, "Is that a fact, *Miss Tarn*? Listen to me child, you'll do well to not go making pacts with the likes of which, you know not."

Victoria shrugs her shoulders as she skips off, "Like I said, she seems like a fine person."

"Never a dull moment."

Free from her high collared shirt and long black skirt, Christian falls back onto her pillow. One arm tucked behind her head, the other suspended before her as she holds up the journal found on the table, titled "*Notes on the Claibornes*, by Elizabeth Lock." With dusk looking on and her tiny window providing a meagre light source, Christian reads with the aid of the oil lamp suspended from her bedpost.

Dear Madam,

I trust my words find you well.

I've taken the liberty of leaving you a few notes, which you may find helpful as you settle into your new post.

My tenure with the Claibornes began a little over four years ago on their Weymouth Estate in Surrey, which is also home to my village. I am of the third generation of Locks to serve the Claibornes. Consequently, I have come to regard the Clairbornes as an extension of my own family and I of theirs, since I've known them all my living days.

My parents were in service to the Claibornes from the time I was a little one. Mr Claiborne assisted my parents in tuition and board for my studies. Naturally, I felt as though there was a debt to repay and returned as their Governess upon completion of my schooling. At this time, Lily Bell had just passed her third birthday and Rosie was still on the breast. Mrs Brooks took to motherhood like a duck takes to water but after the birth of Ash, she hasn't been herself. Both mother and child have fallen in and out of chronic illnesses of one kind or another. Though I have only resided in their Bayswater home for a few months, helping them settle in, I can see Mrs

Brooks growing more poorly by the week. I pray she finds the strength to continue her fight.

Lily Bell and Rosie, on the other hand, are the very picture of health, much like their father. Lily Bell is the eldest, now seven and Rosie age five. Though, if you were to judge Rosie's tenacity, you would think she was the eldest of the two. Lily Bell is not to be underestimated, her quiet nature is only a veneer through which she hides her intelligence from the world, a quality she inherited from her father. Professor Brooks is a brilliant man whose passion for the natural world has enhanced my knowledge greatly.

Christian raises the arch of her left eyebrow.

Now that I'm to be wed, I'll return to my village and begin a family of my own but the Claibornes will never be far from my heart. If I am blessed..." Christian looks up at the cross nailed to the wall above her head, *"...I will one day soon have a family just as beautiful as Prof and Mrs Brooks.*

She giggles to herself as she spreads the open journal across her chest.

With Puddles tucked under her arm, Mrs Claiborne raps furiously on the door to Elouise's apartment. When the response is not immediate, she knocks again. The door swings open causing Mrs Claiborne's knuckles to fly through the air.

"Mother, really. Must you attempt to raise the dead at every turn? Ash has just fallen asleep."

One side of Elouise's sable brown curls has collapsed, leaving her pompadour lopsided. Wearing a rumpled petticoat and long knickers, Elouise sits in front of the unlit fireplace, where she clutches a shawl around her shoulders. Next to her sits her dress, propped up as though she were still in it. In the dim light, the emerald green dress illuminates the deep purple velvet chaise. Her hoop, underskirt, and corset lay on the floor beside the dress.

"Oh Elouise, I wish you wouldn't parade around half dressed. I know you're under the weather but one's got to make the effort to be decent."

Elouise trains a stern eye towards her mother, "You really ought not lecture me about decency. Besides, you know I've been up all night with a sick infant. I had hopes of getting some rest now that Ash is down, which is nothing short of a miracle with you and father shouting down the house."

Mrs Claiborne takes a seat in the armchair next to the dark fireplace, "Well, what am I to do?" Elouise collapses back onto the chaise lounge and throws her feet up on the green dress. "It's for you dear... that I quarrel with your father." Elouise sighs. "Ella, he means to hire that, that black woman. I mean, can you imagine. Well, I for one, will not stand for it. Not in this house."

"I don't care mother."

"What do you mean, you don't care!"

"Please mother, keep your voice down. The only thing I care about is getting help and letting Ash get some sleep."

"Has the world gone mad? Am I the only person concerned for the wellbeing of these children under the tutelage of this, this foreigner. "

"So now you're objecting to her nationality. Father's right, you had no problem hiring an American until you realised she was negro."

"Don't tell me you knew?"

"No mother, I did not 'know'. But I can tell you that I DO NOT CARE."

"Hush Elouise or you'll wake the baby." Elouise rolls her eyes. "It's just that Miss Lock was practically a member of the family."

"Yes, a little *too* familiar if you ask me... and it's no longer Miss Lock, it's Mrs Woods now. Frankly, I'm not sorry to see the back of her, even if the girls miss her. I'm quite keen on getting some fresh blood in here. A new life, a new house, a new perspective."

"You sound just like your father. The man has done this to me on purpose. He insists on punishing me."

"What are you talking about? How is the fact that *my* new governess is a negro woman punishing you! Actually, this has little or nothing to do with you. I agree with father, I think it will be quite novel to have Miss Waters join us. And I couldn't care less what these silly people think."

"Well, we've Georgie to consider. He is not yet betrothed and we cannot afford to sully his reputation with rumours and conjecture."

"Really mother. Georgie? He, above all, will be over the moon to have Miss Waters in our midst and you know it."

Mrs Claiborne falls back into the chair in resignation. Elouise sits up, "Look mother I need help and need help fast. And the girls need their education tending to. We've all read her resume, Miss Waters is bringing a world of knowledge with her. Besides, she's all we can afford!"

"Well, I did advise you against marrying..."

"Don't mother."

"A doctor of plants... well, I never."

"I'm warning you mother."

"Where is he then, our botanist?"

"He's taken the girls with him to the British Museum for a private viewing of an upcoming exhibit, *Treasures of The Great Pyramids*. An old classmate of Winston's, the Egyptologist Samuel Birch, sent him an exclusive invitation. You met him at our Christmas party in..."

"Sorry, I have no recollection of this person. I've had to erase all memories associated with our days at Weymouth. It's all I can do to survive our dreary existence."

Elouise rolls her eyes, "Anyway, this Birch fellow has discovered all sorts of gold artifacts on his latest exploration to Egypt and offered to give Winston and the girls a special tour before the exhibition officially opens to the public."

Mrs Claiborne looks away distantly, "So that's that then. United against me."

"Must you be so damn melodramatic? No one is uniting against you. It will be fine, just wait and see. Give her a chance mother. Is that too much to ask? Once the girls are back, we'll bring Miss Waters down and introduce her. If the girls accept her, that'll be that."

"And if they don't?"

"Then we will put an end to this nonsense." Elouise reclines back onto the chaise and sighs.

Mrs Claiborne strokes Puddles as she casts her eyes on the non-coloured walls. "Ella dear, when are the decorators coming. This dreary room is more than I can bear."

"Tomorrow, mother."

"I assume your husband has finally agreed to the colour."

"Yes, Scheele's green, just as you requested."

"Yes, that's right. All the best..."

"...homes are using it. You needn't bang on about it anymore mother."

A little brass bell above the servants' entrance on the subterranean level rings. Mrs Farraige is in the process of adding chopped turnips, leeks and carrots to the bubbling water around the cow's head. The tinkling bell causes a momentary glance over her shoulder towards the kitchen door but other than that Mrs Farraige continues with the task at hand, stirring the contents of the well blackened cast iron pot.

The bell rings again. "Where is that blasted girl?" She calls out, "All right, all right,".

She hastily covers the pot and wipes her hands on her white apron before opening the kitchen door. Just a few feet beyond the kitchen door a shadowy figure of a man is visible through the frosted glass panel in the front door. Mrs Farraige opens the door to find a man clenching his cap to his chest. A horse shaking its bridle is heard just beyond the black railing of number 7. Her eyes instantly fall to the ground where a battered black trunk sits in the melting snow.

The tremendous weight causes Christian great strain as she levies the trunk upright. First by lifting one end on to the wooden seat of her chair, then by bearing the brunt of the weight on her shoulder as she pushes upwards from her knees. Panting from the exercise, she doesn't wait to catch her breath. Instead, she removes a key ring from a tiny velvet purse. Suspending from the key ring are two brass keys, one big and one small.

Kneeling before the trunk, she uses the larger of the two keys to unlock the trunk. She pulls the two sides open as though it were a giant book. She doesn't fight to contain her glee at the contents as she removes two little packages bundled in brown paper and twine.

Inside the kitchen, on a wooden rack, hangs a row of more brass bells. Dotted throughout the rack are white porcelain labels with swirled lettering indicating different rooms of the house. Most of the bells hang below blank spaces where the porcelain labels have been removed.

The bell marked "1st Floor Parlour" rings. Mrs Farraige looks up from the cow's head, which is now cooked but being shoved into the oven to brown. "Girl," she shouts.

Victoria scuttles in with a broom in hand, "Yes, Mam."

"Mrs Brooks rang for you. I imagine she'll be wanting to see our new governess," Mrs Farraige fights to contain the smirk on her face. "Off you go... and keep your ears open."

"Yes, Mam."

※

"Miss Waters?" Christian fails to answer so Victoria knocks again just as gently, "Miss Waters?"

Christian swings the door open before Victoria has the chance to repeat her performance, "It's Christian. Call me Christian, Victoria."

Victoria takes a tiny step back at the vision before her. Christian has removed her outer clothing and stands before Victoria in her white corset and under clothes. The backlight from her oil lamp casts a halo through her unbraided bushy hair around her head and shoulders. Hanging from her neck on a thin gold chain is a blue glass bead painted with a bright yellow design.

"Yes ma... You're wanted by Mrs Brooks... I'll wait for you to dress." Victoria steps back into the hallway but Christian opens the door wide enough for her to enter.

Once inside, Victoria approaches reaching out her hand, "Can I touch your hai..."

Without equivocation or removing her eyes from the clothes she's about to don, Christian's voice runs cold "You may not". Christian casts her eyes to the floor before turning around to face Victoria and addresses her in a softer tone, "Victoria, I *would* like your help with the fire. When you get the chance." Christian steps into her petticoat.

"Yes Christian."

Victoria busies herself with the task of lighting the fire by shredding old scraps of newspaper before sitting lumps of coal on them. "In the winter, I light fires for the family at four o'clock when they take tea and sometimes at breakfast. First, in the master bedroom for Mrs Claiborne, then study for Mr Claiborne and then the upstairs parlour for Mrs Brooks. But now I just light them whenever they ask. Mrs Brooks has a sick baba, so I light the fire a lot for her." Victoria strikes a long match and uses the flame to ignite the scraps of newspaper around the coal. "Her husband, Prof Brooks, he's ever so nice. He gave Miss Lock, that plant." Victoria points to the periled African violet, "But now she's married so I'm to call her Mrs Woods."

"Ah, I see." Christian smiles to herself.

Victoria rises from the smoldering fireplace to find Christian buttoning the last button around the high white collar of her shirt, covering the little colourful blue and yellow bead. "Thank you Victoria, much appreciated."

Christian blows out the flame from her oil lamp. "Let's go, shall we. I don't want to keep my new employers waiting on my first day." Victoria smiles as they exit but just before the door swings shut Christian doubles back and picks up the two tiny bundles wrapped in brown paper and twine laid at the foot of her bed, "Oh, I almost forgot!"

Even though the daylight has completely diminished Elouise's green dress, which she is now wearing, still radiates in the oil lit room and the glow coming from the fireplace makes the colour look even more magical. Elouise shakes Christian's hand and uses the opportunity to examine the object of her curiosity closely. Like her mother, Elouise's stature is closer to a child, a trait that becomes exaggerated next to Christians towering presence. Elouise eyes search the roots of Christian's bushy hair, the peachy hue of her cheeks, the intensity in the cupid bow of her lips and eventually her eyes, so dark they seem like bottomless wells, which do not fail to catch the scrutiny of Elouise's examination. When their eyes meet, Elouise is quick to cast her gaze away towards her mother. Puddles snarls at Christian. "Oh, shut up Puddles. Don't worry about him, mother's dog doesn't like anyone."

Elouise's energy dissipates as she collapses on the lounge. Not having been offered a seat, Christian remains standing and lays on a thin veneer of a polite smile.

Despite Victoria's best effort to blend into the background, Mrs Claiborne spots her, "That'll be all Miss Tarn." And with that, Victoria shuffles out the door.

Elouise continues her examination, though a lot more conspicuously, "So tell me, how was your journey, Miss Waters?"

"It was uneventful Mrs Brooks, which is more than I could hope for."

"Did you travel via steamship?"

"Yes, the Britannia."

Mrs. Claiborne scoffs, "The Britannia? Surely that was an unnecessary expense. The Great Western would have suited *you* more, I would think."

Christian does not respond but gives only a slight glance in the direction of Mrs Claiborne before returning to Elouise.

"Mother, must you be so crass. I understand the Britannia shortens the voyage by five days and I, for one, am grateful for your early arrival." Christian nods her head in acknowledgement.

"But I must say the journey must have cost you a pretty penny."

Christian is forced to nod once more.

"Why here Miss Waters? Why would you leave New York to come here, surely there must have been suitable employment for you closer to home."

"This is my home."

Both women look on puzzled.

"I mean, my father is English and was raised on a farm not far from here in Hertfordshire, before joining a Quaker missionary. "

"I see. So, your father *is* English."

"Was English. He recently departed this earthly plane."

"God rest his soul. And your mother?"

"Creole. From Haiti. She too has passed."

"I see. So, you would be considered mulatto? Is that the correct term for the progeny of white and negro?"

"Only by whites Mrs Brooks."

The two women recoil and slightly shift themselves in their seats.

Mrs Claiborne begins to fan herself, "Do you mean to say you're a bastard. I believe marriage between races is illegal in the United States, isn't it?"

Without flinching, "My parents were married in Haiti long before they arrived in the United States, mam."

Mrs. Claiborne still fanning, "I didn't know the Quaker church tolerated that sort of thing."

"They don't mam, my father lost his collar but retained his membership in the flock and continued his good work."

Elouise interjects with a slight tremor in her voice, "How long did you live in Haiti before moving to New York?"

"I've never lived in Haiti Mrs. Brooks. I was born in Jamaica, where my father was working with abolitionists. We left Jamaica shortly after The Baptist War "

Mrs Claiborne stops fanning herself and begins a new study of the towering presence before her. Her profile, her jawline, the length and breadth of her nose, the curve of her ear, all begin to bear an air of resemblance. Christian smiles ever so gently to herself.

Elouise continues her line of questioning, "I say, what ghastly business. Do you remember much?"

"No not at all, I was barely two at the time."

"Mother, won't Georgie be thrilled?'

Mrs Claiborne has turned to stone and does not respond.

"Mother!"

"Yes, what is it Ella?"

"Georgie!"

Mrs Claiborne, who is still reeling from the impact of Christian's answers, can do no more than breath as she continues to inspect Christian.

Elouise gives up on her mother and returns her attention to Christian. "My brother George very much fancies himself a renegade and is dabbling in this abolition business. England is out of it now, so I don't see what business it is of ours what the Yanks do."

The tilt of Christian's head causes Elouise to alter her line of conversation.

"He recently completed his Juris Doctorate at the University of London. You'll meet him tomorrow... I suppose. He always leaves early and returns late. These days he's only home to eat and sleep. Wouldn't you agree mother? Mother!"

Mrs. Claiborne is still transfixed on Christian.

Though mystified and a frustrated with her mother, Elouise continues on, "How old are you, if you don't mind me asking?"

"I'll be twenty five this summer."

"And you're not yet wed?"

"No, I was quite intent on continuing my education and becoming a lettered woman in medicine."

"A nurse?"

"No, a physician. But I left my studies to care for my ailing parents."

"I see. What will you do now? It will be near impossible to marry if you don't seek a husband soon."

"Actually, I'm not seeking a husband. I plan on returning to my studies after I take care of a few personal matters."

Muffled laughter and galloping footsteps coming from the front door cause Victoria to pull her ear from the door outside the parlour. It takes her no more than three seconds for her to disappear into the back staircase designated for the servants.

When the door to the parlour swings open Lily Bell and Rosie tumble in. "Gran mama!" The two girls run to greet Mrs Claiborne but freeze in mid-motion when the unknown presence of Christian is detected.

Elouise gestures for the girls to come to her, "Well, you're both excited aren't you?"

Prof Brooks follows the girls through the door and also stops in his tracks as he takes in the vision of Christian before him. He briefly turns to his wife searching for answers to his unasked questions in her face, "You must be our new Governess, Miss Waters?" He pushes himself forward and extends his hand to Christian, who places her hand in his. Prof Brooks returns the gesture with a small yet tender kiss on the back of her hand.

Mrs Claiborne lets out a sigh strong enough to blow the hair on Puddles' head. Any traces of merriment quickly fade from Prof Brooks as he takes the cue and dutifully kisses Mrs Claiborne's cheek, "Mother," before taking his place by his wife's side and tasks himself with another dutiful kiss, "Ella."

Everyone is focused on Christian – including Puddles.

Elouise breaks the silence, "This is Miss Christian Waters, our new governess, girls. Say hello." The elder of the two girls looks to her mother for confirmation, Elouise nods in acknowledgement.

Prof Brooks also encourages the girls on, "Come on girls, where are your manners. Say hello to Miss Waters."

They both sheepishly continue to linger by their mother before the youngest, Rosie, with her father's peridot green eyes and his strawberry blonde curls, approaches Christian. "How do you do?"

Christian lowers herself until she is kneeling before the child but even then, she continues to tower, "I'm well, thank you Rosie. It's lovely to meet you."

Christian hands the little girl one of the packages, "Pour vous."

The little girl glances over her shoulder in the direction of her mother. Elouise gives Rosie a permissive nod. Rosie takes the package. Prof. Brooks prompts his daughter, "Well, what do you say Rosie?"

"Thank you."

"Du rien."

Elouise nudges the elder girl, "Go on Lily Bell." With her maternal grandfather's dark hair and stormy blue grey eyes, Lily Bell hesitantly moves closer to Christian.

"Bonjour Lily Bell. C'est un package pour vous." Christian hands the girl the remaining bundle.

"Thank you."

"Du rein."

As though nothing else is taking place in the room, Mrs. Claiborne interjects, "Really Ella, haven't you the time to curl their hair before they leave the house. They look like street urchins."

This time Elouise ignores her mother, "French? Well, aren't we the lucky ones!" The girls look longingly at their mother. Surrendering, "You may open your gifts."

Lily Bell and Rosie pull the bow of the twine open and remove the brown paper to reveal rag dolls. However, the dolls are void of eyes and all other facial features. Nor hair or clothing. They are just the bare outlines of the human body, stuffed to capacity giving them an eerie life-like quality. The two little girls look to Christian in bewilderment.

"Lily Bell, we're going to give your doll a glorious head of dark hair and blue eyes just like yours. And Rosie, we're going to give your doll pretty little curls and green eyes just like yours. Then, I'm going to teach you how to sew and we're going to make pretty little frocks just like yours. How does that sound?"

Joy lights up in Lily Bell, "That sounds splendid Miss Waters."

"Can I make my doll a yellow dress, Miss Waters?" asks Rosie.

"Yes. You can pick any colour you like." The two girls smile and giggle with each other.

Elouise looks coyly over to her mother, "Thank you Miss Waters, that will be all for now. I'll let you settle in and rest up and we shall reconvene here tomorrow after breakfast."

"Thank you Mrs Brooks, Prof Brooks, Mrs Claiborne. Au revoir mes enfants," Christian makes her way to the door.

Elouise, "Did you have a good time at the museum girls?"

"Yes mother."

As if by flight, Prof Brooks makes his way to the door and holds it open for Christian. She gestures a thank you with a nod to Prof Brooks who smiles on broadly as he watches her exit.

Elouise continues, "Very good. Let's clean up. Supper will be will be ready soon."

Christian, is about to head down the hall leading to the narrow servants' staircase but stops when "Ogechi," is whispered in her ear, though she is surrounded by silence and no one else stands near her. She turns only her head and looks in the opposite direction down the grand staircase behind her. "Ogechi," echoes out from a disembodied voice coming from the shadowy hall below her. She whips her whole body around descends the grand staircase without stirring the air.

Through an open door, Victoria lays out table settings in the dining room. She is so invested in her task that she doesn't see Christian walk by the open door. Adjacent to the dining room is the closed door to Claiborne's study. Again, she hears a woman's voice whispering, "Ogechi."

Christian gently turns the knob and pushes the door open. Like all the other rooms in the house, it is ram packed with overly ornate furniture. In the rear of the room, an oil lamp flickers on the desk lighting the painting of a young Claiborne. She enters, carefully closing the door behind so as not to make her actions known.

After navigating through the sea of furniture Christian stands in front of the desk, where she gets a better look at the painting of Claiborne in his glory. Ever so gently, she touches his hand.

On the desk, next to the lamp, a book lays open. With one hand on the open page to retain its place, she lifts the cover and reads the title before returning it to its original position. She sniffs a glass containing a clear brown liquid and strokes the length of his welled pen. Again, "Ogechi" is whispered in her ear. This time Christian closes her eyes. "Ogechi, look behind you."

Christian turns to face the wall behind her, then opens her eyes to find an enormous oil painting dwarfing the door she just entered. This time she doesn't have to fight her way through the furniture because she is transported in one giant step and stands just before the painting. "Ogechi," it calls.

The painting is of a tropical landscape depicting a plantation at the foot of a succession of hills, both near and far. It is composed of many shades of green, from lush rich palm greens to deep dark moss greens. Centred is an orange grove. The tiny colourful fruit punctuates the planes of green. Black bodies dressed in colourless rags move through the avenues of the grove with giant baskets strapped to their backs, brimming with the little orange treasures. A succession of black bodies head towards carted mules where more black bodies, draped in colourless rags, haul and dump the little treasures. They return to the grove with empty baskets. Dotted around the circumference of the grove are white bodies in broad hats and hemp white shirts, seated in their saddled horses – whips at the ready.

In the foreground, in the lower left corner, a tree stands bearing a different kind of fruit. Its ackee painted to blush with tones of red and apricot. A woman steps barefoot from behind the tree and into its shadow. Her green dress resembles the hills behind her. Her dark skin is barely visible in the shadows but her beauty is unmistakable. Around her neck dangles a brightly coloured blue bead with a yellow swirling pattern.

The woman reaches to pull fruit from the tree. She's on tiptoes but it's still just beyond her grasp. After a little struggle she pulls a ripe ackee off the branch, its skin split revealing the tender creamy fruit and deadly black seeds within. She turns and looks at Christian speaking in Igbo, "Do you remember me Ogechi?" She hands the ackee to Christian.

With tears streaming down Christian's face, "Nne" as she takes the fruit from the woman.

Upon contact of the ackee, the gilded frame around the painting pulls away from the wall and levitates towards Christian. Holding the woman's hand, she steps through it and onto the lush green grass of St. Anne, Jamaica. The woman steps out of the shade and into the sun. She is young, no more than eighteen. Her braids rest comfortably on her shoulders. With her forefinger, she wipes Christian's tears, "My little Chi Chi." They embrace. They stop long enough for the woman to pull from her skirt a little leather pouch tied with a red drawstring and hands it to Christian before the two return to embracing.

In the background a whip lashing flesh is heard, followed by a whimpering cry. Christian pulls away looking for the source of the agony but the woman stops her. She clasps Christian's hand and the two run from the grove. They run fast and they run long.

Down a rutty lane and around a bend. Night descends. A man hangs by his neck. His genitals have been cut away and his naked body bears the lashings of a lifetime. Christian tries to scream but nothing comes out. The woman pulls her on to continue. The man's body is undoubtedly lifeless but his eyes follow Christian as she passes him.

The two women continue on down the lane and into a barn where bales of hay are stacked in the loft. Men, maybe four, maybe five, their hemp white shirts stained with grime and sweat, stand by cheering on another man who is raping a girl in colourless rags - she's no more than twelve. She and only she sees Christian and the woman. Her eyes follow the women as they walk just feet from her. As one man finishes, another begins but they remain oblivious to the presence of Christian and the woman.

Outside, Christian falls to her knees, her sobs are violent and silent. When she turns to the woman, she finds her gone.

A two-story white house glows in the dark. It's guarded by a succession of columns on either side of the front door. They support a balcony that runs the width of the building. Just beyond the white house, Christian sees the woman in the green dress trying to run but she's limping. There's a man behind her. He is faster and stronger and easily catches her by placing her in a headlock. She bites his forearm and is temporarily free of him. But his anger has now grown into a rage and with it, slaps her to the ground where he then kicks her. She screams as he mounts her, kneeling on her arms and whispering in her ear. He pulls a knife from his hip holster and places the blade firmly along her throat and cuts the blue and yellow glass bead from her neck. He rips her dress away from her chest.

Christian tries to come to the woman's aid but finds her foot tethered by an iron cuff and chain, though the chain itself isn't tethered to anything at all.

A flicker of light shines from the handheld lantern as Claiborne runs out of the big house. He is younger, slimmer and has a full head of black wavy hair as he did in the old oil painting behind his desk. He leaves the lantern on the porch and uses both hands to finish securing his breeches as he runs to melee. He pulls the man off the woman by the collar of his shirt. The man falls back and scuttles away in the presence of Claiborne.

In an attempt to preserve her dignity, the woman tries to re-assemble her dress. Shaking his head Claiborne attempts to help the woman to her feet. She recoils. On a bended knee, he extends his hand once more. She looks into his eyes but is distracted by something over his shoulder. She points in horror. Claiborne turns to find the man back on his feet and banishing a log. He ducks out of the path of what might have been a deadly blow and quickly rises to his feet. In one mighty punch, he knocks the man back down. Claiborne picks up the log and stands over him, where he sees that his ring has made contact with the man's cheek leaving a bloody gash. The man cowers as he braces himself for impact but Claiborne throws the log back down. He turns to face the woman, she too is now on her feet.

Claiborne tucks the woman into his embrace. As they pass Christian, the woman whispers in Igbo, "Ogechi, get the bead." Claiborne neither sees or hears this exchange as he and the woman ascend the stairs leading to the big house but not before she stoops to pick up the lantern. The door slams shut behind them.

Cupping his cheek, Christian watches the battered man stumble away into the darkness. The iron clasp around her ankle snaps open freeing her to rush to the scene where the woman fought for her life. In the darkness, Christian runs her hands along the ground until she encounters the black leather strap with the blue and yellow bead in tow. She holds it close.

Rain. Rain pours all around her but the fire of the men and women coming down from the Cockpit Mountains has not been extinguished. Like lava flowing from a volcano, the amber streams of their torches flow from the green hills of St. Anne and consume fields and buildings in their path.

The morning's mist mixes with the night's smoke. The many shades of greens are no more. Just charred trees and red streams. It is in one of these red streams that the woman in the green dress lies face down. Beside her, a little golden brown girl stands crying. A man in colourless rags picks her up and runs. He runs fast and he runs long.

In a room, the little golden brown girl sits at a table, her feet far from the ground. A middle-aged woman with a similar complexion attempts to feed her porridge but is distracted by a conversation taking place on the patio beyond a set of French doors. She leaves the child at the table and stands by the billowing curtains at the entrance so that she can better hear the conversation.

The child is barely old enough to feed herself but hunger and self-preservation kicks in and she reaches for the spoon.

Claiborne's wavy hair is in total disarray and his breeches are stained with blood and mud. He towers over a tiny framed man with a white collared shirt and black waistcoat but then breaks down and sobs before the man. Now it is the little man who towers over Claiborne. Behind them, wisps of smoke still blow around the air. The man places his hand on Claiborne's shoulder and pats him reassuringly.

The little girl topples the porridge to the ground and with it begins to cry. The woman is quick to come to her aid but is brushed aside by Claiborne. He kneels before her, "Do you remember me Ogechi?"

Christian, turns to face Claiborne in his study, he stands just inside of the door, "Yes, I remember you... father."

Nightshade

The weight of the dark purple curtains cause Victoria to struggle as she ties them back with gold tasselled cords. A hazy grey light seeps into the dining room through a set of giant sash windows. From the sideboard, she lifts out a stack of floral decorated plates and one by one, lays them around the table covered by a white tablecloth with an elaborate lace trim.

Mrs Farraige cracks eggs into a mixing bowl. She stands over the kitchen table, looking up through the subterranean window and is blessed with the occasional set of feet jetting by.

While the exterior of Christian's trunk is plainly adorned with brass tacks outlining the black paint, which is chipped and scrapped bearing the cedar frame, the trunks interior, in stark contrast, is delightfully ornate. The left side of the trunk is reserved for hanging items, as evidenced by a number of white blouses, a black dress, black skirt and a petticoat suspended from slim cut cedar hangers. Below, a compartment is reserved for shoes. The right side of the trunk is myriad of draws in varying sizes fastened with tanned leather straps designed to keep them in place during transit.

Still in her nightgown, Christian kneels before the upright trunk. Only the crown of her head is visible over the top of the trunk. At first glance, it appears as though she is in prayer and the contents of her trunk the subject of devotion. Upon closer inspection, she is bustling away with contents of the trunk. She closes one of the little drawers and fastens the leather strap. With the strength of her inner core, she rises from the kneeling position, in her hand a little leather pouch tied with a red drawstring. It is identical to the pouch given to her by the woman in the painting, whom she called 'Nne'.

"Morning all," Georgie enters the subterranean kitchen through a set of swing French doors as though he was entering a saloon in the wild west. Instead of encountering a bar of gunslingers, he is faced with the surprised looks of Mr Fen, Victoria, Christian, and Mrs Farraige, who answers for the group as she rises from the kitchen table where they are all seated.

"Can I help you, sir?"

Everyone else at the table also rises in his presence but Georgie's eyes are fixed on Christian. "No, that's all right Mrs Farraige." Georgie looks down at their bowls of porridge in white bowls striped with a blue rim, "Sorry to disturb your breakfast but I simply couldn't wait a minute longer to say hello to our new governess." Unable to take his eyes of Christian he strides mightily until he is by her side. "I must say, it's absolutely marvellous to meet you." Georgie extends his hand to Christian, "How do you do? I'm George Claiborne Jr."

Christian rests her hand in his and he kisses the back of it. She nods her head in acknowledgement, "A pleasure to meet you, sir. I'm Christian Waters."

Georgie looks up from Christian's hand to the rest of the staff who are still standing and watching him with their jaws slightly dropped, "Where are my manners. Please do take your seats."

In a flash, Georgie vanishes through the swing doors and the staff return to their porridge. But just as quickly as he disappears, he reappears with a chair, one that matches the set at the table. He resumes his conversation with Christian in pitch-perfect French, reflecting his fine level of tutoring, "I hear you are fluent?"

Much like Georgie, Christian's French is of the highest calibre, "Yes, sir."

"I assume you received your primary education at the African Free School in New York?"

Christian chokes a little on the spoonful of porridge she's just taken in and struggles to swallow it down without giving away her shock at Georgie's line of questioning. "No sir, I received my primary education at the Friends' School in Manhattan. It's run by The Quaker Society."

"Oh right, your father was quite active with the Quakers, wasn't he?"

"Yes, that's right."

"The Friends' School is highly regarded, why not list it on your resume?"

"I didn't see the need if I'm listing my university studies."

Though the rest of the occupants at the table are unable to understand the conversation, Mrs Farraige decides to interject, "Are you sure I can't fetch you something to eat Mr Claiborne?"

Without taking his eyes off Christian, "I assure you Mrs Farraige, I'm quite all right." Georgie resumes his private conversation in public under the guise of French, "I see. If I recall, you completed your coursework at Oberlin College but no degree?"

Christian wipes the corner of her mouth with a napkin from her lap and rests the spoon along the rim of her bowl, "That's right, sir."

"Well, why not? Why go that far and not finish?" Georgie looks around the table and realises by the intensity of the faces mirrored back at him that he's slipped out of French and into his mother's tongue.

"Christian remains in her mother's tongue, "Immediately following my mother's death, my father fell ill. I left Ohio and returned to New York to care for him, though it wasn't long before he too passed."

"Shame."

"No shame at all. It was a small price to pay for a man who did so much for me."

"Of course. How insensitive of me. Will you return at some time to obtain your degree?"

"Yes, I should like to one day but there are a few matters for me to address first."

Nodding his head in agreement, "Of course. Yes, of course," but his brows knit in befuddlement as his voice trails off. His attention returns to the other participants at the table. They're going through the motions of eating but not actually consuming any food. "God, how rude of me. I shall make myself useful elsewhere."

Georgie rises to his feet and begins to make his way out the door with the superfluous chair in hand but stops and turns once more to Christian in French.

"Listen Miss Waters, I meet, along with other members of The Coalition to End Slavery, every other month at the Freeman's Club House. I would be honoured for you to join me... us at the next meeting, which will be in a fortnight."

Christian looks on stunned, unable to even blink.

Georgie lets out a quivering laugh, "Come, come now. Cat got your tongue?"

"Well, I'm not sure if that would be permissible... with my duties here."

"Leave that with me."

"Yes, sir."

Georgie exits the kitchen through the same set of swing doors, "Bon appetite everyone!"

The clinking of the cutlery is deafening in the amplified silence at the kitchen table. Christian keeps her head down as she steadily spoons in her porridge but remains highly aware of the trained looks in her direction.

On the ground floor, in the formal dining room adjacent to Claiborne's study, Victoria lays out a covered tray containing scrambled eggs, a rack of toast, marmalade, and a tea service on the sideboard. Georgie sits at the table noshing on an apple while reading a large leather-bound law book with gold embossed lettering.

Claiborne is the next in and though he seems to not be aware of Victoria's presence he greets her just the same, "Good morning, Miss Tarn."

"Morning, sir." With a brief curtsey, Victoria disappears into the servants' staircase through a hidden door in the panelled wall.

Claiborne takes his seat at the head of the table and buries his head in the newspaper he has just removed from under his arm. "I trust all is well with you, son?"

"More than all right father, I just met..."

The clicking of the approaching heels to Mrs Claiborne's boots is enough for Claiborne to clear his throat loud enough to drown out the rest of Georgie's commentary. Upon entering the dining room, Mrs Claiborne's eyes pierce through the newspaper Claiborne attempts to hide behind.

"Morning mother."

Mrs Claiborne's eyes do not stray from the invisible bull's eye painted on the raised newspaper at the end of the table, "Yes, good morning Georgie." She takes her seat on the opposing end of the long table.

Dust has not the time to settle before Prof Brooks, Elouise and their two little girls file in. Elouise addresses her father, "Good morning father." She effortlessly leans into the tiny space between him and the newspaper and plants a little kiss on her father's cheek.

"Morning dear," Claiborne's intense focus on the print remains steady but his eyes fail to move back and forth across the lines.

The little girls take their seat alongside their mother, placing the elder of the two, Lily Bell, next to her grandmother and opposite her Uncle Georgie, who playfully greets them with a poked tongue. They both giggle and mimic him.

Prof Brooks dishes two plates of scrambled eggs and toast for his daughters, and then the same for himself and wife before taking hold of Ash and then takes a seat opposite her in between his father-in-law and brother-in-law. He dutifully acknowledges the heads of the household, "Morning, sir. Morning, mother." Neither fully respond and instead mutter something vague.

After biting his apple down to the core, Georgie heads over to the sideboard, "Mother, can I serve you?"

"No thank you Georgie, I feel a bit uneasy this morning."

"Father?"

"Ah, no thank you, son."

Georgie beams all the way back to his seat with a serving hearty enough to compensate for his parents. "Ella, I just had a little chat with your new governess. You were right!" As he gives her a wink.

"Right about what exactly?" snarks Mrs Claiborne.

Since Georgie has already stuffed his face with a heaping pile of scrambled eggs and toast, it is Elouise who answers, "That she is an excellent choice for the post. What else could we be referring to mother?"

Mrs Claiborne looks towards her husband, who is now peering above the newspaper watching the discussion between his family. Mrs Claiborne manages to catch his eye, "I trust you had a good night's sleep sir?"

"I did, dear wife," he returns to his newspaper.

"Is that so? Well, I did not! Not that you inquired."

"Oh? You're discontented. What a surprise," still talking from the innards of his newspaper.

"Do you mock me, sir?"

"I dare not!"

Georgie looks up from his breakfast having just barely swallowed his food, "Won't it be absolutely thrilling to have an American so close at hand...though, there's that American chap, Geoffrey something or the other... but he is little more than a buffoon. I mean, how could you not want to get a fresh perspective of what's going on in the world with revolution beckoning at every turn. Especially in the United States. Why just the other day, I..."

Mrs Claiborne interjects, "My son, you have been misinformed. Do you not know our new governess is not actually American..."? Georgie looks puzzled. His mother continues, "... She's Jamaican!"

Georgie rests his knife and fork on the plate before him, "Well, I never." After a second of self-reflection, he snaps back, "No matter mother. Miss Waters has studied in New York and Ohio and spent the better part of life in the Americas, so for all intents and purposes, she's

American. Her Jamaican origins only enhance her... her... cosmopolitan sensibility, don't you think?" Georgie returns to the hills and valleys of scrambled eggs on his plate.

Mrs Claiborne's eyes have yet to leave her husband's newspaper, "Ella, didn't that woman say she was about to turn 25?"

"Yes, I believe she did."

"Then definitely born prior to 1831, wouldn't you say?"

"Your powers of deduction are amazing, mother."

Prof Brooks turns to Georgie, "I say old boy, wasn't 1831 the year of the slave insurrection in Jamaica?"

Georgie takes a moment to ponder, "Why yes, I do believe you're right! Do you suppose Miss Waters has any recollection?"

Claiborne drops his shield by way of his newspaper, "Listen, let's not set about bothering Miss Waters with such matters. She's not here as some sort of sideshow to satisfy our curiosities. Besides, she was only an infant during the uprising and left the country shortly after. So how could she possibly remember anything of significance."

Mrs Claiborne scowls at his comment.

Undeterred, Claiborne continues, "My dear wife, surely you're not going to lay the blame of the slave rebellion at the feet of Miss Waters. And before you start, nor is it her fault we lost the plantation."

"No, I don't suppose I can blame her for either of those incidents but I am wondering how you know when she left Jamaica?"

The entire table turns their focus to Claiborne, including little Ash. "You, uh. We...well her references clearly state she was schooled in the United States, so she must have left as an infant."

"Do they Mr. Claiborne? Because last I checked she made no reference to her primary education. Or, did she mention this while in your chambers last evening?"

"Well come to think of it, MAYBE SHE DID!" Claiborne's immense presence seems infinitely larger as he juts out of his chair and slams his beloved paper on the table.

Mrs Claiborne too rises out of her chair though her height difference remains relatively the same, "DON'T YOU DARE SHOUT AT ME!"

"Mother please," Elouise rests both elbows on the table and props her head up with her hands. She uses her napkin to wipe the beads of sweat from her brow. Her damp armpits darken her emerald green dress.

Claiborne returns to his seat and to his paper, "Steady on, old girl."

Mrs Claiborne remains on her feet, "Why is everyone in this family against me!"

"No one is against you mother, I simply am not feeling well."

Georgie turns his attention to his sister, "I say Ella, would you like the fire out. You look like you're roasting."

"Don't trouble yourself Georgie, I'm going to head up for a lie down before the decorators arrive."

Mrs Claiborne finally succumbs to her seat, "That's right dear. You rest up. We'll take our little therapeutic walk this afternoon." She returns her attention to her husband only to find herself resuming a conversation with the newspaper at the end of the table, "Perhaps our finances will see you take waters in Bath soon?"

A disembodied voice from the newspaper speaks out, "Yes, we'll try to sort something out. Though, that quack Moss seems to be charging a pretty penny. And all for the instruction to take magical walks."

"Yes, Dr Moss charges a pretty penny. That's because he is the best physician in this backwater."

Prof Brooks deliberately jumps into the fray, "I say, is there any news on the Bank of England robbery."

Georgie gratefully obliges, "No, only to confirm that the blast was set off after they escaped the vault."

"But I just don't understand. Why go through the trouble of breaking to steal just the two gold bars, when the vault is filled to capacity and then announce to the world what you've just done."

Elouise fans away. Georgie leaves the table and turns to the fireplace behind him. With a set of cast iron tongs, removes lumps of glowing coal from the hearth and relocates them to the grill.

Mrs Claiborne also leaves the table but to ring the velvet rope in the corner, "Georgie leave that to Miss Tarn."

"I can manage mother."

Mrs Claiborne returns to her seat "It's not a question of whether you can manage or not, it's a question of how low your father is going to let us sink. Look at you, you're blackening yourself. That's all we need. We've already one nigger too many in this house."

The thunderous crash of china and flatware hitting the floor reverberates throughout the house.

Claiborne stands in front of his overturned chair with the tablecloth in his hand. He and all else at the table are wearing one or more items from breakfast, while dishes and cups are strewn about the floor. The two little girls and baby Ash burst into tears but all else have been stunned quiet. Georgie rises as though he was in slow motion from the hearth of the fireplace. The only other movement in the room is the dripping of spilt tea running off the table onto the oriental rug below.

Also frozen in mid-action is Victoria on the servants' staircase heading up to the dining room, Mrs Farraige with a ball of dough in her hands and her eyes cast up to ceiling, Mr. Fen with a black tinted paintbrush in his hands at the front door.

Christian smiles broadly as she continues to clean the remnants of white chalk from the blackboard.

As Christian heads up the narrow staircase leading to the servants' quarters she stops at a small round window in the middle of the landing. She looks up and out at the moon. Its brilliant blue-white light casts a silvery halo around it in the misty night air. The moonlight also casts a cross over her face, caused by the shadow of the quartered window panes of glass.

She stands and stares a little longer before retreating into the darkness. When she steps back out into the moonlight, she is in the backyard of number 7, the yard she has only ever looked down on from her window.

"It was a full moon like this when I first met your mother. As a matter of fact, if the moon hadn't called me on to the veranda that night, I might not have had met her at all."

Christian doesn't move, not even to blink.

"I see you are drawn to the moon too. I hope you take comfort in knowing where this trait comes from. I do. I see much of myself in you. It's quite remarkable how blood works. From my mother to me and now to you. That's where you get your height. And Georgie. We're a family of giants!"

Claiborne emits a chuckle before striking a match and lighting his pipe. The orange glow gives away his exact location in a dark corner of the garden. He now steps out into the moonlight and stands by Christian. "Not Elouise though, she takes after her mother. Bless her."

Claiborne puffs away.

"I see your mother in you too. She was so beautiful. And smart. Most unlike anyone I've encountered in my life and I imagine in the next. She knew everything there was to know about plants and their medicinal properties. What she couldn't cure, she could heal. I never heard it from her lips but it's said she came from the dark continent as a little girl. Stolen from her village and sold to the British for a few lumps of sugar at a tender young age. They say she came from a powerful line of miracle workers and your mother certainly had the gift."

Claiborne puffs away.

"I see Anna and Rev Waters did right by you. Or, you wouldn't have reached this height and be this bright. Nor would you be here if they'd taught you to hate me. God knows I've hated myself for giv... leaving you with the Waters. But when I saw your name on the resume, I knew it was you and that you couldn't possibly hate me. Why else would you find me and come here?"

Claiborne's hypothetical question is met with silence. The silence and stillness are punctuated only with the puffing and whirling smoke coming from his pipe.

"How did you find me Chi Chi?"

Silence.

"Well, that's not important now. What's important is that you're here, with me. Safe and sound."

Silence.

"I've never felt so at peace. My family... you're everything to me."

Christian lets out a deep sigh, "From your payments."

Claiborne removes his pipe.

"I found receipts in your name from a bank here in London. I also found the letters you sent..." Christian turns to Claiborne. "...to my father. Asking about me. What was I doing? What subjects I had taken on. How..." She turns back to the moon. "That's how I found out who you were. But as you said, none of that is important now."

"Were you angry when you learned the truth?"

"Not at all. I was loved. My parents never lied to me, I always knew I was adopted. They only tried to protect me. They told me all about you over the years and never spoke an unkind word. They told me how you supported me. Paid for my schooling and made an effort to show that you cared, even if from afar. I didn't find your letters and bank notes until after my father died."

"I'm so happy you were loved. That you've had a good life. But most of all, I am happy you're here. You have no idea how much my heart has ached for you Ogechi."

Christian lets out another deep sigh. She turns to walk away but he grabs her arm.

"Do you hate me Chi Chi? I mean, do you think you could love me...too?"

"What was her name?"

Confusion strikes Claiborne's face.

"My mother, what was her name? My parents knew nothing of her. Only that she gave me this." Christian pulls out the little blue and yellow bead from under her high necked white blouse.

Claiborne takes a tiny step back at the sight of the bead. "I'd forgotten you have that, it's been so many years. Yes, she wore it always." With an outreached hand, he takes a tiny step towards her but Christian tucks the bead back into her blouse.

It's now Claiborne who lets out a sigh, "Katherine. Her name was Katherine but I've heard her people call her Emuesiri. They say it was her name before she was taken to Jamaica. Though I only ever heard that name from her lips once."

Christian pulls her arm away and proceeds to exit the garden.

"I didn't want to give you away but as you can see... things just .... I'm sorry things couldn't be different."

"Good night, sir."

Claiborne remains behind, alone in the moonlight. The little orange light in his pipe fades to black.

"Do you miss living in New York?" Rosie's mittened hand is cupped by Christian's gloved hand, still marred by the black paint rubbed off the railing on her arrival to Craven.

"No, not yet Rosie. But I've only been here a couple of weeks. Let's see how I feel in a couple of months!"

Lily Bell, who holds the other of Christian's hands leans forward and over Christian's body to talk to her little sister, "Why would she miss New York? Her mummy and daddy are both in heaven so we're her family now. Aren't we Miss Waters?"

"I suppose you could say that Lily Bell." Christian's smile warms away the chill in the midmorning air as the three walk along Craven Hill towards the 'Residents Only' garden square. Christian tests the surface of the railing, ensuring the paint is dry, before pushing the gate open.

"Have you ever seen a Red Indian?"

"I have Rosie. Plenty of times."

The two girls are so wrapped up in Christian's revelation that they are oblivious to the reaction from fellow garden dwellers. But not Christian, she keenly observes their flint etched faces. Their stern loathing stares.

Inhaling deeply, Christian looks up to the dark grey clouds. The wind suddenly picks up pace causing her to hold onto her bonnet in an effort to keep it on. Clouds fly across the horizon giving way to patches of blue and flickers of light. She is still fighting to keep her bonnet on when she exhales.

Gusts of wind whip sand around her black ankle boots as she ascends the rickety wooden planks making up the shoddy staircase leading to a general goods store. Her little hand is firmly gripped by Rev. Waters' hand. In his other hand, the brown leather grip initialed 'LSW'. His trouser leg blows ferociously, as he struggles to keep his round rimmed black hat on with both hands occupied. The fact that his white collar keeps flapping in his face further complicates matters. Christian wears a white dress and stockings. Two long corn-braids stretch down her back, fastened with red and white gingham ribbons, all of which have also taken flight.

"We don't serve your kind in here."

A set of steel blue eyes peer out from a red-faced man of diminutive stature behind a wooden counter. He is addressing a large framed man. Time has caused his back to bow but his two salt and pepper plaits still rest there with pride and almost reach his waist.

"It's just a loaf of bread."

The red-faced man pulls a sawed-off double-barrel shotgun out from what seems like nowhere, "Look here, you red skinned nigger, I ain't gonna tell ya again. Now git."

"Were you afraid Miss Waters?"

"Terrified."

The large man now stands erect, even though it is a struggle for him. He slams a loaf of bread on the counter and walks out past Christian and Rev Waters.

"Did he try to chop your head off?"

Christian looks down from the sky to Rosie who seems so far away - like a dot below her.

Lily Bell interjects, "She means scalped."

"What! Girls, why would you think such a thing?"

The red-faced man stashes the shotgun back into its magical hiding place under the counter. "I'm sorry about that sir. My brother was found shot in bed as he slept and I just know it was them damned Shoshone bastards. How can I help you?" He does a double-take when he discovers a little brown girl hiding behind her father legs.

It only takes a couple of steps for Rev Waters to reach the counter. For the little brown girl, it feels like miles. Rev Waters picks up the same loaf of bread the other man put down and places a coin on the counter, "I'll just take this bread."

"Mister, you must not be from these parts. "

"No, home these days is Brooklyn, New York."

"Well, I'll look the other way this time but the girl stays outside next time."

"I see. Thank you for your notice sir."

The red-faced man pulls the coin across the counter with his index finger and lets it fall into his open palm. As Christian and her father exit the store, the cash register let out a ping causing her to look behind. The red-faced man glares back at her. He closes one eye and pulls an imaginary trigger with his real finger.

"Miss Lock said that any people that don't have Christ in their hearts are savages. And that white settlers will have to fight to save the souls of Red Indians from their heathen ways."

Rev Waters looks down the dusty road. First to his right, then to his left. He spots the large framed man. "Come on Christian." But she doesn't run alongside him. Instead, she stands behind a nearby wooden hitching rail and watches her father run after the man. When Rev Waters reaches him, he removes his hat and hands him the loaf of bread. The man refuses it and keeps walking. Mr Waters hands it to him again. The large man pauses for a second and then accepts the bread with a tip of his hat. Rev Waters watches him walk away a little before replacing his hat.

It takes a little effort but eventually, Rev Waters finds his daughter's hiding place. He picks her up and plants a large kiss on her cheek. He holds her close as they continue in the opposite direction down the dusty throughway.

"No Lily Bell, Miss Lock is quite wrong." Christian kneels down to the children, ensuring eye to eye contact. "It is the American Indians who are fighting for their lives, their land and for their very existence. Anyone who can't see that could never call themselves a Christian."

This baffles the children.

"I know. It's a very complicated matter but we'll have plenty of time to talk about this and much more in the months to come."

"Years! Years to come."

Christian smiles, "Well Miss Lock was right about you Lily Bell. You are as smart as a whip. Yes, years to come."

※

Though the trees are bare, Christian helps the girls identify them by the distinguishing patterns on their bark. All the while, the other garden inhabitants file out exchanging bitter remarks between each other. The girls remain blissfully unaware as they rediscover the garden.

The trees are all quite young, except one, a great oak in the corner of the garden. Just below it, on a bench, sits a man of advanced years with salt and pepper hair and matching beard and moustache. He is wearing a shiny top hat and a wool coat with high collars, the thick black fleece lining visible. In the vacant park, the man's presence becomes more noticeable to Christian. She never leaves his watchful eyes. This causes her to turn her full attention to him. The two remain locked in an unflinching stare down. It is he, who first breaks the tension by rising from the bench. He places his weight on a silver knobbed walking cane as he gains his balance. Christian braces herself.

The man is about two feet from her when he removes his hat, "Good afternoon, mistress."

"Good afternoon."

"I'm Robert Browning," Browning pauses in anticipation. After blinking his eyes a few times, followed by a blank stare, he decidedly replaces his hat.

Christian rises to her feet, Browning tilts his head up ever so slightly as she extends her hand and the two exchange a gentle shake, "Christian Waters."

"Ah, an American."

"Yes, newly arrived."

Christian returns to her seat. "Please," she gestures for Browning to join her. He accepts her invitation.

"How wonderful. I hope you don't mind me intruding but what brings you here."

"My work. I'm a governess." Christian points to the girls who are still playing merrily among the garden's shrubbery.

"Aren't they the Claiborne's children?"

"Not exactly. They belong to the Elouise and Prof Brooks. Elouise is daughter to the Claibornes."

"Ah, I see. They're, quite new to the area too, aren't they?"

"That's right. But isn't everyone?"

"Ha! Yes, I suppose. I'm a guest of the Claiborne's neighbours, the Flower-Adams. I' hope you don't mind me saying but you remind of someone. Someone very dear to me and I miss her very much."

"Gone from this world?"

"I'm afraid so. You see, she was my grandmother, so she's been gone for some time now. But seeing you today has brought her alive again. Thank you."

Christian smiles on.

"Well, I shan't keep you any longer. It's been a pleasure, my dear girl. Absolutely delightful. I'll let you settle in but I hope you'll join the Flower-Adams and myself for supper one of these fine evenings."

"That's very gracious of you. I would like that very much."

With the aid of his cane, Browning rises up from the bench and tips his hat "Hopefully our paths will cross before then."

Christian smiles broadly and nods her head as Browning makes his way down the path and out of the garden. His figure fades away but Christian's smile remains.

From her window Christian studies the night sky. She clutches her shawl tightly around her shoulders. On the little round table behind her, the oil lamp burns next to the open journal left by Miss Lock

Through the reflection in her window, Christian watches the door behind her slowly swing open and the figure of a tall man appears within its frame. It's Georgie, dressed in his outerwear with his hat in hand. He immediately looks over to the empty chair at the table and then to bed. It's a few seconds more before he notices Christian standing by the window. Her presence unnerves him and he takes a little step back as his body jolts in fear. When she turns to face him and he clears his throat in an attempt to pull himself together. "Fetch your cloak," he whispers softly.

"Why?" She does not whisper but she does not speak loudly either.

"I'm taking you the abolitionist club I mentioned a fortnight ago."

"Thank you but I don't think so."

Georgie steps into her room and gingerly closes the door behind him. Christian remains in place. He approaches her slowly and stops just before her.

"Miss Waters, I would like to insist that you come but I understand that I can't force you," he says with a whimsical smile.

Christian nods her head in agreement.

"Listen. To be perfectly frank, I think this would be mutually beneficial for both of us."

"Oh? How's that?"

"For starters, many Friends of the Quakers Society will be there. And I hear the theatrical talent Ira Aldridge is in town, so he most likely will be there."

Christian throws her shawl on the bed and swings her cloak around her shoulders as they exit her room.

"Then there's this affable chap called Charles McGhee who will almost certainly be there along with some of the greatest minds of Black Britain."

As they float by Mrs Farraige's door it gives the slightest creek as it is pried open. The sound tickles Christian's ear. Instead of turning to confirm the source, she engages her peripheral vision.

"Then there's us lot," he says with a wink.

They sail down the narrow servants' staircase.

Outside Georgie puts his hat on, which causes Christian to stop in her tracks. She tilts her head at the sight of him.

"It's a new style called a bowler. Do you like it?"

With a quick nudge, Christian pushes the back of the hat forward causing it to be cocked slightly to one side.

"I do now."

Georgie smiles and gestures to the waiting carriage. He extends his forearm and Christian uses his firm frame to steady herself as she steps up. He climbs in after her and closes the little black door. After a knock on the cloth covered roof, the driver slaps the reins over the horse's arse and the carriage pulls away.

The curtain in Claiborne's study falls closed.

Sometimes gently, sometimes violently, the carriage rocks back and forth over the cobbled road. Christian takes in the view of Hyde Park, though only the outline of trees is visible in the moonlit sky.

"Just there is where the gallows of Tyburn stood." Georgie reaches across Christian and points to the clearing at the corner of the park, just before they proceed down Oxford Street. "I'm proud to say that as a nation we no longer see public executions as a means of entertainment or an effective deterrent against crime. The judge I clerk for was the chief proponent for the removal of public executions."

"Instead, executions are hidden behind prison walls? If executions are an unjust form of punishment, why not abolish them altogether?"

"You make a valid point, but it's a step in the right direction. All journeys begin with one step, no?"

"I suppose."

"Poverty is rife in London, that's what drives a man to a life of crime. No gallows will deter an act of desperation. The dichotomy between the haves and have-nots is deeply entrenched and readily visible, though too few from my end of the economic spectrum prefer not to see it. I imagine

I might be tempted to become a bit of a Jack the Lad or maybe a Dick Turpin if faced with watching the starvation of my family. That's how we Claiborne men are cast. We fight for our families and for those who cannot fight for themselves."

"Your sentiment is noble for sure but it is easy to speak of fighting while seated in a comfortable chair. The battlefields are strewn with dead soldiers because of men that find it easy to speak of fighting. Trust me, sir. You've no idea what starvation feels like, nor do you know what the Claiborne men would do if their family was suffering."

Georgie's frustration mounts as he tries to refute Christian, "Mr. Fen came to us, his tongue ripped from his head and a host of other injuries endured after an explosion on a gunner boat during the Anglo-Chinese war in service to the Crown. Like many men of his background, he lacks the capacity to read and write. With his post-war injury, he was left with only a series of gestures to communicate and not a penny to his name. When Fen came to my father begging for bread, he could have tossed him a shilling and left it at that but he saw something in him, a spark of hope, I suppose. So, he brought him into his employ. Why, Miss Tarn had all but been abandoned from the time she was an infant. Shuffled from workhouse to workhouse, all with ailing health. She was not long for this world when my father found her peddling wilted flowers on the side of the road. And now look at the flourishing young woman she has grown to be. As for Mrs Farraige, she fled Ireland during the potato famine. A childless widow, who experienced extreme anti-Irish prejudice and difficulty securing employment without valid references but we employed her none-the-less. With the money earned during her short tenure in our household, she sponsored her only other kin, a brother I believe, to come to London, who is now gainfully employed himself. So no, I have never faced starvation but I have... we have helped those fighting it. There are more kind acts to mention but there's no need to sound like a braggart."

Christian's attention is no longer on the view from her carriage window but is solely focused on Georgie. Save the clip-clop of the horse's hooves hitting the cobbled road, silence befalls the carriage's interior.

"Do you know if the same kindness was extended to the hundreds of men and women enslaved on your father's orange plantation in Jamaica?"

Georgie hangs his head, "He inherited that plantation from my mother's father. It is a system that he did not create."

Christian looks on, her appetite for a suitable response unfulfilled.

"He struggled with the idea at first. He knew it would not be possible to sell it. So when he gained the inheritance, he travelled to Jamaica for a couple of years to ensure the workers were treated well..."

Christian returns her gaze out the window to the shuttered shops on Oxford Street.

"...as well as could be expected under the circumstance. He's not perfect, I know. Not one of us are. He is simply on a journey – one step at a time."

"Yes, one step at a time."

The raucous noise of the gathering oozes out from the open windows of a terraced Georgian townhouse. So loud and gregarious is the banter that it is heard before the carriage carrying Christian and Georgie comes to a full stop.

Christian stands at the bottom of the stairs examining the grand exterior of the red brick building, "Is this it?"

"It is. Not what you were expecting?"

"No, not exactly. I was expecting something more of a sombre affair. It sounds as though there's a celebration in full force in there."

"Yes well, what you hear is the sound of extroverts but please don't mistake the nature of two hundred strong men... and women. We will not win this fight with the squeaks of mice but with the roars of lions."

"I suppose."

They ascend the small staircase leading to the Georgian townhouse. Before entering, Christian takes in the view. "Is that St. Paul's Cathedral?"

"It is. So, this is your first time visiting the City of London?"

Christian nods.

"This is the old part of town. One day, I'll have to give you a proper tour."

"I would like that, thank you."

From the ceiling to the floor, the lobby is covered in panelled wood. Just a few steps in a receptionist sits before a ledger.

"Name?"

"Mr George Claiborne Esq."

"Name?"

"Miss Christian Anna Waters"

"Are you able to make a donation to the Freedom Fund tonight Mr Claiborne? Miss Waters?"

"Oh, yes."

Christian pulls a coin from her small velvet purse.

"Mr Claiborne?"

He too pulls several coins from his purse and hands them to the receptionist.

"Thank you. Cloakroom to your right."

The lobby is a hotbed of activity. Georgie and Christian steadily bustle through the crowd. An elder statesman with a handlebar mustache and wire rimmed spectacles taps Georgie's back, "Good to see you, Georgie my boy. Save a little time for me for a quick chat."

"I shall, sir."

Georgie takes Christian's hand and pulls her closer to him, "May I introduce Miss Christian Waters."

"Well, it's a pleasure to meet you, young lady."

"Miss Waters, may I introduce my mentor, the Right Honourable Sir Arthur Riverton."

"It's a pleasure to meet you too...Sir Arthur?"

"Yes, that's right my dear. An American? From which state do you hail, if you don't mind me asking?"

"I've lived in several places before calling New York City my home."

"Really? How wonderful. Georgie boy, I see you're playing host tonight. Let's catch up some other time."

"Yes, sir."

"My dear Miss Water's, I look forward to our next encounter."

"Yes, as do I."

They continue to make their way through the crowd. Georgie leans into to her ear, "That was the judge I mentioned. He is the most brilliant legal mind in England and he's on our side... and I clerk for him." Georgie smiles on proudly.

It's a few more steps before they hear a voice calling from yonder. "Miss Waters. I say, Miss Waters. Christian and Georgie scan the room both near and far but to no avail. "Up here, Miss Waters." They look up to a balcony and find Robert Browning in a league of gentlemen of his ilk. He lifts his top hat in acknowledgement. Christian smiles and waves, while Georgie returns the sentiment by lifting his bowler hat.

Georgie looks on in wonderment, "You know Robert Browning?"

"Yes, we met in the park. So, you know him too?"

"I only know of him. He's lauded as one of the greatest poets of this day and age."

Christian smiles on proudly.

※

A flame flickers to and fro Mrs Farraige's face as she holds a candle stemmed in a little brass holder to the line of her vision. She places the candle on the table next to Miss Locks' journal and the African violet before bending down before the trunk. She pulls it open, ever so gently.

※

Voices in the great hall bounce around the room carried by the high ceiling, before whirling around Christian and penetrating her ears. It's a heady mix of baritones filling the core, lifted by tenors and grounded by bass. Christian steps away from Georgie and into a symphonic universe of men.

"Does this belong to you, Madame?"

A voice speaks softly into her ear. So deep is his voice that her body vibrates from within. The stray hairs around the base of her neck dance in the breeze caused by his hot breath and tickle her. Christian's eyelids involuntarily close as her eyes roll back. Feeling the rest of her body also falling backward, she fights her way forward and opens her eyes. She turns to face the owner of the virile octave and finds herself face to face with a man to match that voice. Almond shaped eyes, a widow's peak framing his face, and warm cinnamon brown skin, which sets off his deep blue suit, and white ruffled shirt.

"Madame?" The man extends a white handkerchief delicately decorated with embroidered blue flowers.

Christian's heart races as she struggles to find a response. "N-no, it's not mine."

"My apologies."

Detecting the Patois in his French accent, Christian responds in a language known to inhabitants of the Caribbean, "Thank you for asking."

"You are Haitian?"

"My mother."

The man smiles, "As was mine. Do..."

Before the man has time to finish his response, Georgie makes his presence known by standing in the non-existent space between the man and Christian, causing his chest to come painfully to close to the man's, "Good evening, sir."

"Good evening."

Georgie and the man stare at each other for far too long.

The man's friend, who until now had been content to stand in the background, steps forward. He is of the darkest of hues and his cheekbones are so high and sharp they cast contrasting white highlights against his smooth ackee seed skin, "Good evening, sir. We seek only the owner of this pretty handkerchief. It wouldn't be you, would it?" The two men give a little smirk.

"It is not mine, nor that of the woman in my charge." The two men bow their heads and retreat.

"I shall have to keep you close, I see. This world is full of scoundrels and grifters ready with ploys like lost handkerchiefs."

"I don't think they had any ill intentions."

"I beg that you see past dandy attire and into the true nature of intent."

"I shall soon be twenty-five and as a woman of years, I assure you that I am both experienced and weary in the latent malevolent character of men."

Georgie nods his head in agreement but then cocks his head to the side. "And benevolence. We're not all snakes in the grass." He winks at Christian.

She smiles back, "No, I suppose not."

The man stands with the handkerchief still extended from his hand. His eyes have not left Christian though her back is to him. A woman approaches him, "Oy, that's my handkerchief!" He smiles politely and hands it to her. He turns to find Christian has vanished into the crowd and is gone from his view.

※

At the podium, an elderly white man in a black Quaker clergy suit and white collar addresses the gathering, "Brothers and sisters, thank you for your attendance this fine evening." The audience applauds. "This morning I woke to find daylight streaming through my window. What a pleasure it is to wake in the morning light once more, after months of darkness. It is in darkness that evil prevails and in light that it perishes. Let us be that light which shines on the abomination known as the enslavement of our brothers and sisters on distant shores."

The audience cheers in unison, "Hear, hear."

"I take great delight in bringing you an update in the case of our brother, Joshua Glover. I have received word from the Liberty Party that the fearless act of our brother Sherman Booth has forcibly freed brother Joshua from the Milwaukee jail after fleeing Missouri to seek asylum in Wisconsin. Brother Joshua is now safely residing in Canada."

Applause waves in and out of the crowd.

"You will be pleased to know that we have almost reached our target fundraising goal to permit the passage of twelve more souls fleeing the tenacious grasp of the American Fugitive Slave Act. I recognise the faces of many beneficiaries amongst the audience. I am pleased that you are safe and well, and with us tonight."

Another round of applause, cheers, and whistles erupt throughout the great hall.

"Before we get on with tonight's business, we're delighted to receive a negro spiritual from Mr Ira Aldridge."

A portly man of average height ascends a raised platform adjacent to the podium. The corners of his stiff upright collar disappear into his bushy sideburns and dig into his cherub-like cheeks. He lowers his head to the master of ceremonies and then again to the audience.

"Good evening all. I am grateful for the care and attention given to my brothers and sisters in bondage. There isn't a day that goes by that I don't recall the same horror from hell that is here on earth in the form of slavery."

"Hear, hear." rumble throughout the gathering.

"I am also grateful to be here with you tonight."

Christian, gently cranes her neck and looks around the room without turning the rest of her body. Her searching eyes are met with the man in the blue suit. They are already fixed on her.

"Lord, I keep so busy praising my Jesus."

A melody, rich and deep, fills the room. Christian whips her head around to find the unlikely source the voluminous voice coming from Ira Aldridge.

Speckled throughout the crowd a choir comprised of ebony, mahogany and, pine coloured faces join in, "Keep so busy praising my Jesus"

Tears roll from Christian as she joins them, "I keep so busy praising my Jesus, ain't got time to die."

Georgie returns from the cloakroom with their outer apparel. He hands Christian her cloak before he is greeted by a fellow member, "Georgie old boy, how have you been keeping yourself..."

With Georgie fully occupied, Christian exits the crowded lobby to the pavement below the staircase. Feeling the nip in the air, she swings her cloak around her shoulders creating a black curtain around her body. When the cloak sweeps across her face a man is revealed before her. A most curious little fellow. Due to his bowed back, his height is difficult to gauge. His attire is comprised of the finest cloth ever made but each item is threadbare and harkens to the years of a bygone era. His skin is rich in walnut tones making his bushy white afro glow.

"Good evening, Miss."

"Good evening, sir" Christian extends her hand. He receives it and lays a gentle kiss on the back of her hand.

"I'm Charles McGhee but everyone just calls me McGhee"

Christian cocks her head slightly, "And I'm Christian Waters... are you Jamaican Mr McGhee?"

"I am indeed."

"As am I. Whereabouts exactly?"

"From Shiloah in the foothills of The Land of Look Behind, where St Catherine's borders St James and Trelawny."

Joy washes over Christian's face, "I too, come from a plantation on the north coast near Ocho Rios, St Anne, but I left shortly after The Baptist War. Sadly, I was quite young at the time and remember almost nothing of my infancy in Jamaica."

McGhee now shares the same confounded expression. He takes Christian by her forearms, "Mi gone too long. Mi take to the seas with the Navy to support mi family. Mi do it for mi dem. Mi sen every penny back home. Mi nuh know of the uprising until it was too late. Too late. Mi miss the war I should have been fighting for, instead mi a go foreign to fight for people who nuh care for we."

The two embrace. McGhee looks up in time to see Georgie approaching. He hurriedly, yet inconspicuously places a folded piece of paper into her palm, "For you."

"McGhee, how are you?"

"I'm well sir and trust you are too"

"I am in fact. I see you've met Miss Waters."

"I have Mr Claiborne and now I must be off."

With that, McGhee bows to Georgie and then to Christian. Though with Christian, his head lowers but his eyes remain fixed on her. And she on him. As he continues down the road, he places his top hat on his white afro. As with the rest of garments, the hat is just as fine, just as worn, and just as dated.

While Georgie summons a carriage, Christian steals a moment for herself to read the note. 'Jean-Luc Saline' in large swirly lettering is all that is on the paper.

"Christian," George calls her from the steps of the black cab. She quickly refolds the paper and tucks it into her purse. Before climbing into the carriage she takes a last look over her shoulder at the townhouse. On the steps, with his foot planted firmly on the back of a stone lion, Jean-Luc Saline looks on. His friend, nearby, lights a hand rolled cigarette. Christian climbs in but Georgie, noticing the men, remains focused for a while longer before he too, climbs in.

"I hope you don't mind that I use your Christian name. I don't know why but I feel so at ease with you?"

"And I with you... Georgie."

As the carriage pulls away, the two men descend the staircase and watch Christian and Georgie descend into the night.

Sprawled out on the floor of the drawing room Lily Bell and Rosie are engrossed in the task of making dresses for their naked dolls gifted by Christian. The dolls now look more human, resembling each of the girls; Lily Bell's has the Claiborne dark hair and blue-grey eyes, while Rosie's has the Brooks strawberry blond curls and bright green eyes. Cuttings of sherbet coloured fabric lay around them. Christian leads the way showing the girls stitch by stitch how to assemble the tiny garments.

A shrilling scream rings out from number 7 Craven Hill Gardens.

Christian stops short at the sound of the distressed cry but Lily Bell reassures her, "I wouldn't trouble yourself if I was you," then returns to sewing.

Claiborne rolls his eyes and continues reading his book through the powers of a magnifying glass. Mrs Farraige also expresses annoyance and sucks her teeth as she continues stirring the contents of a large blackened Dutch pot on the coal burning stove. Mr Fen barely registers the scream and continues screwing a brass "7" onto the black shiny door. Prof. Brooks, who is mopping sweat from Elouise's brow turns in the direction of the front door to their apartment but doesn't rise from his seat. Elouise attempts to rise up but Prof Brooks gently pushes her back down into the comfort of her pillow.

"Grandmother is always screaming Miss Waters," Rosie adds, who has so immersed in her needlework her tongue hangs from her gaping mouth.

Lily Bell chimes in, "Grandfather says she's mysterical."

Christian's ear is still trained towards the door as silence besets the house again. "I think the word you're looking for is *hyst*erical." She is about to return her attention to her dressmaking instruction when another scream rings out.

This time all inhabitants of the house, save Elouise, drop what they're doing and rush to the source of the audible SOS at the base of the stairs. There, in a purple and green checkered pool of a collapsed hoop dress, lies Mrs Claiborne. Puddles stretched out at the hem of her dress.

Victoria stands over her with a bucket in one hand a scrub brush in the other. It is *her* scream that has summoned everyone.

Christian and the girls are the next to meet the vision followed by Mr Fen who takes his place by Victoria. The little ones call out for their grandmother as Christian holds them back. Claiborne dashes to her side but is beaten by Prof Brooks' strength, youth, and agility. He shields the body of Mrs Claiborne from Claiborne's outstretched arms. "Sir, I beg you not to move her. After a tumble down the stairs adjusting her position might do more harm than good."

Christian returns with girls to the drawing room. Tears run freely over their reddened cheeks as Christian asks, "Lily Bell, look after your sister. I'll be right back." She then closes the door behind herself but doesn't move much further from it.

Prof Brooks checks for a pulse on her wrist and then her neck. "Yes, yes she's alive," as he answers a question, no one has spoken aloud.

The plump hand of Mrs Farraige reaches across Prof Brooks line of vision. In her grip, a tiny cobalt blue bottle stopped with a cork. Mrs Farraige pants heavily as though she had just competed in a five mile foot race and not a dash up a flight of stairs. She struggles to speak, "Smelling salts, sir."

Prof Brooks shakes the bottle with great vigor before pulling the cork out and waving it under Mrs Claiborne's nose. Almost immediately, her eyes start to blink until they fully open. A collective gasp is heard from everyone. Everyone, except for Christian who remains silent and distant, in front of the drawing room's white panelled door.

Mrs Claiborne stirs on the ground until her eyes fully open. The first thing she sees is Prof Brooks, then beyond him, Christian. Mrs Claiborne tries to speak but her words are jumbled. Prof Brooks offers his forearm, which she uses to pull herself up, though she hasn't realised that her husband is behind her aiding her to a seated position. Prof Brooks tries to comfort her," Steady on mother, you've had a tumble down the stairs and..."

The upright position gives a new strength to Mrs Claiborne, "What nonsense are you talking about? I did no such thing."

"Well, what's happened then?"

The voice coming of her husband causes her to whip her head around. Tears well in her eyes as she points to the white ball of fluff at her feet.

All eyes turn to the dog. Prof Brooks leaves Mrs Claiborne's side to tend to the dog. He does little more than pick up the head and drop it back down, "She's right! It's dead!"

While everyone is focusing on the dog Mrs Claiborne focuses on the figure of Christian in her plain, black, unhooped dress, with white collar. Christian does not look away and their eyes lock firmly. "You did this!" The group now follow the line of vision from Mrs Claiborne to Christian. "You black bitch."

"Not this again, Ivy." Claiborne needs the aid of the banister to pull himself up and then stands beside Prof Brooks blocking Mrs Claiborne's view of Christian.

But Mrs Claiborne wiggles her head from side to side until she ekes out a vision of Christian, "Get out. Get out of my house."

Christian retreats into the drawing room, where on the other side of the door, the two little girls rush to her side and cling to her black skirt revealing her white petite coat. Christian, "No need to worry girls, your grandmother is well." She kneels down and wipes their tears with a handkerchief pulled from the cuff of her sleeve.

Lily Bell's lips quiver as she attempts to speak, "Why is she so horrible to you? You're not going to leave us, are you?" Lily Bell's line of questioning causes Rosie to cry harder and hug Christian's tighter. Christian pulls the girls closer and the three lock in an embrace. "Don't worry girls, I'm not going anywhere," she kisses the sides of their heads. Then in a softer lower tone, "... not just yet, anyways."

They attempt to return to their needlework but struggle not to be distracted by the shouting coming from the hall.

Dark grey clouds rush past the moon causing flickers of light to bounce off the window panes behind Christian. The strong wind also blows her skirt so hard that the outline of her legs become visible. Her braids, too, have taken flight and dance around her head. Like a monolith, Christian stands steadfast impervious to the elements. Before her, a little bump in the ground covered in black earth and marked by a small white cross bearing the name of "PUDDLES." Her hands are covered in the same black earth, as is the little leather pouch with a red drawstring removed from her trunk weeks ago.

A whiff of tobacco whirls around her nose. Without moving much more than her hands, Christian tucks the leather pouch into the waistband of her skirt and without raising suspicion of her actions, she wipes the soil from her hands.

"She wasn't always like this. There was once a time when she was lovely, so full of joy. But life has let her down. I've let her down."

With the exception of the whipping wind, there's only silence.

"I think she knows."

"Knows?"

"About you. Well, at least she suspects."

Silence.

"She definitely knew about your mother. The trade winds brought rumors and gossip back to the shores of England faster than the cargo ships. It damn near killed to her know…

"…that you had taken up with a black woman?"

"No, though I understand why you would arrive at that conclusion. It damn near killed her to know that I loved your mother. Actually, it most certainly did. She had changed so completely by the time I returned. Barely recognisable. I honestly believe that it's not the loss of income or status that makes her so bitter today. It's the loss of love. And for that, I'm to blame."

Silence.

Claiborne moves closer to Christian and stands behind her. "Look at the girls, how quickly they've taken to you. And Georgie, he is most certainly proud to have you in his company. Ivy…. well she just needs time to adjust. I'm glad you're here and hope you'll stay. But make no mistake, this is your home regardless of what anyone else has to say. This is where you belong."

The instant his large hands clasp her shoulders, she pulls away.

"I wish you a good night sir, I must make my way back to the servants quarters."

Her white petticoat catches the moonlight as she exits the garden.

Nemesis

Tiny white flakes of chalk crumble away, creating a cloud around Christian as she scribes the alphabet across the blackboard. First the capital letters, then the lower case.

Victoria enters the drawing room, "Good morning, Christian."

"Morning Victoria."

Tucked under her arm, Victoria carries a small bundle wrapped in newspaper. She lays it on the tiled edge of the fireplace.

"It looks like we'll have some sun today, so I'm sure a fire won't be necessary in here."

Victoria looks out the window to the dark grey cloud covered sky. "Are you sure, mam?"

Christian stops writing and focuses solely on Victoria.

"I'm mean, are you sure Christian?"

"Quite sure."

"Ok, I'll just clear yesterday's ashes then"

Victoria removes the outer sheets of the newspaper bundle, leaving enough to keep the package of coal intact. Then with the brass shovel and pan hanging next to the fireplace, she collects the charred remains in the fireplace but every once in a while, she glances over to Christian writing on the board.

Christian smiles to herself, "Would you like to have a go?"

"Go?"

"A go at writing on the board."

"Oh no thank you Christian."

"Come on. Have a go. We both know you want to."

"Well, I don't know how to.... I can't read nor write. I'm as dumb as they come."

Christian stops writing and focuses on Victoria, "Nonsense. You've just never been taught, is all. Where I come from, Negros are told that they lack the capacity for a formal education but nothing could be further from the truth."

"No thank you, just the same."

"Come here Victoria. What have you got to lose? This is a blackboard! You couldn't make a mistake if you tried!"

Victoria rises from the fireplace, where the soot forms a dusty black cloud around her. Christian breaks her stick of chalk in half and hands Victoria a piece.

"Let's start at the beginning. This the letter A." Victoria copies Christian's strokes, "First a diagonal line from south to north, followed by another line in the opposite direction from north to south, then a horizontal line across the midsection of the two lines. Voila! And what's this letter called?"

"A?"

"Well look who's reading and writing! That was quick!"

Victoria's smile reveals every tiny tooth in her head. Before her smile has time to fade the sun beams in through the window. Victoria's eyes squint as she turns to face it.

"Next, the letter B."

First Christian stands, then she sits and then she stands again. The clock on the mantle in the drawing room chimes indicating the hour of nine o'clock.

It takes several knocks on the door to Elouise's apartment before there are any signs of life coming from within. The latch slowly slides across the door before it's cracked ajar. Lily Bell, still in her nightgown, peeks out. She purses her lips and places her index finger on top of them before speaking to Christian, "Shhh, mummy's still sleeping."

Christian nods in agreement and then pushes the door wider open, allowing for her entrance. She is only a few steps into the apartment before she is struck immobile. The parlour where she first met the girls a few weeks ago, which was a standard off-white, is now ablaze in several shades of green. The room glows, despite the curtains being drawn. Even after Lily Bell closes the door behind her, the interior still generates an unnatural radiance.

"Where's Rosie?"

"She's in our bedroom playing with our dollies."

"Have you eaten?"

"Yes. Miss Tarn brought us eggs and soldiers."

A dry raspy cough floats on air down the hall.

"Go play with your sister."

Lily Bell's bare feet leave behind the sound that only a child can make as she runs along the parquet tiled hall. Christian ties back the purple velvet curtains in the glowing green parlour and cracks the sash window open causing the white net curtains to float on the breeze. She lowers her nose down to the fresh air and inhales as much of it as she can.

Even in the daylight, she is still alarmed by the intensity of the room. The bright green wallpaper is textured with darker green velvet flowers. She runs her fingertips over the flowers and smells them. The odor causes her brows to knit. At this moment, she catches her frowning image in the large gilded mirror over the mantle. Her clothes have never looked so black.

Another bout of dry rasping coughs breaks out tearing Christian away from the reflection of herself. She unties her bonnet and unlatches her cape as she exits the parlour. She lays them over Elouise's purple chaise lounge but then backtracks and takes them with her after a wary look around the room.

On route to the door sourcing the coughs, she peeks through the sliver of an opening to another door to find the girls merrily playing with the dolls she made them, despite the shelves of fine china dolls around their room. This brings a reassuring smile to her face.

Christian continues down the hall and gently raps on what could only be Elouise's bedroom door. A faint "Yes" comes from within. Christian enters to find Elouise propped up in her brass bed, pillows packed behind her back. Her sandy brown hair is matted and lifeless making it look darker than usual as it hangs over her tiny body.

"Oh, Miss Waters do forgive me. I seemed to have overslept. Please give me a moment, I will have the girls ready for you."

"Please Mrs Brooks, don't trouble yourself, I can see you're not well. I'll tend to the girls."

Christian notices the cradle next to Elouise's bed, "How's Ash?"

"He's stopped taking the breast, I guess it's just as well. But he doesn't seem to be too interested in the milk Mrs Farraige prepared for him either."

Christian looks at the bottle topped with a rubber nipple on the bedside table. What must have been homogenised milk has now separated, giving way to cloudy watery looking substance on the bottom and a layer of white chunky matter on top.

"Where's Prof Brooks?"

"At work. Oh, who am I fooling...in case you've not yet deduced it, my husband is essentially unemployed. We live off his meagre stipend as a researcher at the Royal Botanic Gardens, where I'm sure he would prefer to reside."

"Can I bring you anything?"

Without equivocation, "Time."

Christian steps in further, until she is by her side.

"I fear the worse. I feel my body shutting down function by function. I know I'll not see my girls flower and my little acorn to an oak tree."

"Is there nothing more your doctor can do?"

"Yes, he can help himself to more of father's money. Money that he doesn't have. God knows decorating my parlour put him over the top. Mother..." Elouise's coughing returns and she struggles to regain a breath. She runs her fingers through her hair, "Look it's coming out in clumps now and my sores are getting worse."

She raises her nightgown to reveal a skeletal like frame and a torso covered in red and black lesions. Christian yanks the curtain open allowing for clearer vision but Elouise squirms in the bright light.

"I'm sorry to see you suffer so but do not give up. There's hope yet"

A gurgling sound comes from the cradle. Christian picks up Ash and finds the same red and black sores on the palms of his hands and soles of his feet, though not as advanced as his mother's.

"Mind my girls, Christian. I know I haven't the right to ask, we're little more than strangers but please look after my girls. They've taken an instant liking to you. I thought that after the saintly Miss Lock left, they would never take to anyone else but they took to you as if you were family."

"And I to them."

Christian passes baby Ash to his mother.

Despite a brilliant sun, the wind blows cold. The combination of which, turn the girls' cheeks bright pink. Christian holds their hands tightly as she crosses Porchester Road towards Paddington Library. After pulling the great wooden doors open, she ushers in the girls before she herself enters the grand lobby.

While she peruses the directory, clerks behind the checkout counter murmur amongst themselves as they watch Christian. But it is Lily Bell who watches them. They are about to climb the grand marble staircase at the end of the hall when a call echoes off of the cavernous ceiling.

"Madam."

Christian turns to find a balding man of middle years approaching her. His black jacket and pinstripe trousers add brilliance to the gold chain linking to his pocket-watch.

"Madam, may I be of service?"

"No thank you, I'm fine."

Christian returns to the ascent of the staircase but is stopped again.

"Madam, I must forewarn you. You are free to read anything in the library but that is it. All material must remain on the premises."

Lily Bell interjects, "That's not true. I came here before with my other governess plenty of times and we always took books home."

The man lets out a nervous laugh, "Well, I am sorry but that's the only accommodation I can offer at this time."

Christian nods in agreement, "I see."

She turns once more and heads up the stairs with the girls in tow and does not look back at the man who remains to watch her climb the stairs.

In the stacks, she removes an enormous leather-bound book, its pages yellow and curled. It is so heavy that she is unable to lay it on the table without a thud, releasing a little cloud of dust. The three of them cough and wave their arms in protest to clear the air in front of them. Rosie struggles to see the table top, so Christian picks her up and sits her on the table next to the book. Lily Bell eagerly looks on. Christian removes a white cotton handkerchief from her sleeve and wipes the embossed lettering on the cover, *King's Poisons and Cure All's.*

She runs her fingers down the table of contents before stopping short about three quarters down the page. She then peels away at the huge pages until she finds what she is looking for, "Gotchya!" With a cursory glance over her shoulder, she rips the page from the book causing the girls to gasp. She places her index finger over lips and gives Lily Bell a wink. She smiles and winks back at Christian. Christian folds the sheet of paper into four squares and places it in her bag along with the soiled handkerchief.

With the spirit and sharpness of the waiting wind, they exit the library. The man clad in the black suit does a double take as they pass the clerk's desk. Lily Bell smiles on proudly into the waiting sun.

※

"Nah luv. You'll be needing a proper plant shop, we just do flowers. Check along Westbourne Grove, there's bound to be some decent plant shops along there." A man removes his cap to wipe the sweat from his brow with a well-used handkerchief.

"Will do sir, thank you."

With a nod to Christian, replaces his cap and returns to hoisting crates of cut flowers onto a horse-drawn cart.

※

A little bell tinkles as Christian and the girls enter a plant shop filled with potted ferns on pedestals, orchids in glass cases, and an assortment of plants best suited for a warm climate.

Lily Bell exclaims, "That's a sago palm."

"Well done, young miss" an elderly woman emerges from the back room. Her high collard blouse is met with a broach at the neck. An oatmeal knitted shawl wraps around her shoulders and crosses over her bust before being tucked into her long skirt. The brown of her eyes bled into the white a lifetime ago.

"How did such a little pip come to know so much?"

"From my father, he's a botanist."

"He's my daddy too!" Rosie interjects, "See, this is a Boston fern."

"Oh, very good."

The old women smiles in places where deeply etched wrinkles have formed on her face. She turns to Christian and struggles to retain the warmth in her smile. "How can I help you, miss?"

"I'm, looking for an aloe vera."

Lily Bell chimes in, "It's a succulent?"

"Well aren't you clever clogs but you're plum out of luck. We had a fine specimen but it sold a few days ago."

"I see. When do you expect them back in stock?"

Shouldn't be too long, a month or two."

"I really need one now. Do you have any suggestions for other plant stores in the area?"

"American?"

"Yes, that's right."

"Really? From whereabouts exactly?"

"New York... mainly from New York but I've lived in several places."

"I've always wanted to go but never could and now..."

"Yes well, about the aloe vera?"

"Listen, tell you what I could do." The woman disappears into the back room where she shuffles around pots and tins, then lets out a big 'Oooo," causing Christian and the girls look nervously at each other.

The woman re-emerges carrying a large fat aloe vera leaf, "This was knocked off the plant we just sold. I thought I'd take a stab at propagating it but why don't you have a go at it instead."

Christian's eyes light up in wonderment. "I'm speechless. Thank you so much. How much do I owe you?"

"Tis naught but a leaf."

Christian rummages through her coin purse and pulls out a penny, "Here, this came from America. Hopefully, you'll make it there one day."

Now it's the woman's face that really lights up, "Why thank you kindly."

Christian and the girls are about to leave when she stops short at the door. "You wouldn't happen to know where I could find a sea buckthorn bush, would you?"

"Oh dear, no I don't. My specialty is in plants of the tropics. It would have to be right under my nose to know where anything is in these parts."

"Thank you just the same."

"I say, young lady, why don't you try the gypsy camp. They'll point you in the right direction. Just half a mile or so up the road."

"I will. Thank you again."

The bell over the door tinkles as they exit.

The woman smiles at her American penny, "Well, I never."

Once they step off the curb of Westbourne Grove and onto the soft earthen ground Lily Bell breaks free of Christian's grasp and runs to open the gate leading to a meadow. Rosie follows her sister and skips off into the tall grass.

The three head to the distant corner of the field where a group of caravans is camped under a cluster of giant trees. A dog runs to greet them. It barks furiously.

Christian too barks, "Girls stay where you are". She continues on without breaking her stride.

The dog stops briefly to sniff Lily Bell but continues on to Christian. She lays her hand open for it to inspect. Now familiarised, the dog wags its tail and heads back to the camp.

"Move on girls but no running."

With each step, the ornate details of the caravan become more apparent. Though well weathered, the flowery hints of yellow, pink and green still come through. Carved embellishments provide elegant frames around the windows and doors. Washing hangs from lines strung between the caravans and smoke billows from a wood burning stove standing just beyond the caravan's shadows.

As the three approach, a stream of children of varying sizes file out from between the dwellings. A man and woman appear in the doorway. They study Christian's approach carefully but she has yet to break her stride.

She stops at a little yellow ladder leading to the doorway of the caravan where the man and woman stand, "Hello."

The man, whose jet black hair is indented with a ring around his head revealing that he has only just recently removed his hat, is the first to respond. "Yee."

"I'm wondering if you can help find this plant." She removes the folded paper from her purse and points to a rendering of little orange berries clustered with linear shaped leaves.

The man steps down, his boots so scuffed that it is impossible to determine the original colour. His clothes, dirty and ragged, his tawny tanned skin is deeply creased. He takes the paper from Christian, his fingernails outlined in the blackest of soot.

After examining the piece of paper, he speaks with certainty but his words do not register with Christian.

"I don't underst..."

Obliged to assist, the woman attempts to join the effort. She is done drying her hands on her apron and releases it to fall from her waist. In doing so, she covers the only clean area on her dark burgundy dress. She tucks a loose lock of raven black hair behind her ear, as she speaks. Christian is unable to discern what she is saying either.

The woman now addresses the man and waves her arm towards the trees behind her. The man responds to her and nods. He sets off in the direction that the woman gestured and indicates for Christian to follow with a tilt of his head.

"Oh... thank you". As Christian passes the woman, she nods her head, "Thank you".

The woman responds with a smile, "Yee."

The children of the campsite follow suit and take turns in examining Christian by running across her path.

Fading light bounces off of the water as it gently flows downstream. Nearby, in a clearing of the wooded area, the man stops by a bush bearing little orange berries.

Christian, "Yes, yes... that's it." Christian beams, "Thank you. Thank you ever so much."

In the place once occupied by Puddles, Ash sits on his grandmother's lap. His poorly supported head hangs limply.

"These blasted fresh air walks are doing no good. Enough with quackery of this backwater doctor, Moss hasn't a clue."

"But he's all we can afford."

Mrs Claiborne shoots her husband a fiery look, "Why just the other day, you thought him to be a waste of money. Yet, now you seem content with his services. Ella needs proper medical advice."

Claiborne raises his eyebrows and inhales as though he is about to object but decidedly lowers his brows and exhales.

"So, you'll find the money George. Can you not see our daughter's life depends on it?"

Claiborne surrenders with a succession of nods. Mrs Claiborne is about to exit his study when Victoria enters carrying a tray containing a wedge of meat pie. The congealed yellow jelly packed between the crust and meat jiggles as she walks.

"Will you not be dining with us tonight George."

"No dear, I've some matters to tend to."

"Can it not wait until the morning?"

"It cannot."

Mrs Claiborne continues out.

There isn't space for Victoria to lay the tray on the desk. It is cluttered with an array of papers, journals and books. As Claiborne clears a spot for his meal, he partially uncovers the bold lettering on one of the documents before him, which Victoria sees and attempts to read, 'LAST WILL IN TES...'

In one hand, Christian carries a pillowcase. With the other hand, she uses the wall to guide herself through the darkness of midnight down the servant's staircase. Down and down, until she reaches the final floor of the subterranean kitchen.

She places the pillowcase on the stained and scared kitchen table and searches amongst the pots and pans on the utility shelf until she comes across a small stone pestle and mortar, and a little blue teapot. From a slated wooden block, she pulls out several knives until she finds a small paring knife.

The meagre light source provided by the gas lamp coming through the street level window is sufficient enough for her to navigate through the unfamiliar territory of the pantry.

She grinds generous pinch of rock salt in the mortar. She then places a handful of the sea buckthorn berries on top of the salt. It's a matter of seconds before they're crushed, creating a paste.

By running the knife along the edges of the aloe leaf, she removes the spiky thorns. At the base of the leaf, she peels one of the corners of the skin and inserts the blade. The removal of the skin reveals the translucent flesh of the aloe. She then holds it by the tip and fillets the flesh into the mortar.

On the stove, Christian picks up a blackened kettle and shakes it but it's empty. "Damn," she whispers to herself. She stares pensively at the water pump for a few seconds before taking a deep sigh and pushing down on it. She winces at the clanking pipes as water gushes from the spout and into glass jar she's placed to catch the water.

Mrs Farraige's eye's bolt open, then drop back down. She turns in her bed, the springs squeak under her weight. On her nightstand, a half empty bottle of whiskey and empty glass.

Christian dries the utensils in her employ and carefully replaces every item, excluding the teapot. With a last look over her shoulder, she exits oblivious to the little orange berry on the floor just under the table.

Lily Bell, in her night clothes, opens the door to Christian carrying the little blue teapot.

Mrs Farraige lowers her head in prayer but with the use of her peripheral vision surreptitiously watches Christian, "God, thank you for the meal we are about to receive. May it nourish our bodies and feed our souls. Amen."

Mr Fen, Victoria, and Christian join with an Amen of their own. The four raise their heads and tuck into their bowl of porridge.

"Why Miss Waters, I couldn't help but notice how close you've become with the Claibornes in such a short time. Here it is, not quite two months and you've already made yourself quite at home."

Christian politely nods as she swallows down mouthfuls of porridge. Victoria and Mr Fen look back and forth nervously, as though they were watching a death-to-the-end tennis match. Christian hurriedly finishes what's left of her porridge, then excuses herself from the table and places her breakfast bowl in a pan of water on the draining board.

"Oh, Miss Waters, before you leave, you wouldn't happen to know how I came by this in my kitchen, would you?"

Christian glances over her shoulder and finds herself stunned immobile at the site of a little orange berry in the palm of Mrs Farraige's plump hand. Christian's nervous eyes dart up to find Mrs Farraige's scrutinizing eyes already firmly fixed upon her.

Victoria also bears witness to Mrs Farraige's locked glare, "Oh, I... believe that's my doing Mrs Farraige. Remember I told you about the raven I saw picking the guts of a dead pigeon yesterday. Well, I used them berries to chase it. Made me sick, the sight of it."

"I don't see how that's possible seeing as how I scrub clean these floors every night, as I did last night. Yet, there it was plain as day on my clean tiles this morning."

Christian continues to make her way out of the kitchen without comment.

"Miss Waters, no one uses my kitchen without my permission and that teapot you've got is to be returned immediately. There's no food to be taken in your room, not unless I say so. Them's the rules of this kitchen."

"Mrs Farraige, last I checked the teapot along with this kitchen are all property of the Claibornes and not yours. I shall take as many meals in my room as I please. As a matter of fact, from here on in, I will be taking all of my meals in my room. If you find fault with my actions then your gripe is with Mr Claiborne and not with me. Good day to you."

Victoria struggles to retain her smile as the door swings shut behind Christian.

In her tiny room, which is not big enough to house a table and chair, Victoria sits on her bed. With her newly found dexterity for holding a pencil, she writes "VICTORIA" over and over. The lines are a bit shaky but there's marked improvement with each rendition. She then starts on a new word, "WILL". It's almost perfect.

Blinding but only for a split second, a flash of light quickly fades, leaving a trail of smoke which takes much longer to dissipate.

The glare of the white light gives way to Elouise, sitting propped up on the purple chaise-lounge in the ever-glowing green parlour and her ever-glowing green dress. So bright, so vivid is the green that not even the field of white flowers surrounding her could dampen the hue. Her white skin looks like buffed porcelain next to the dress. The red cherry stain on her cheeks and lips offer the perfect high notes for this symphonic explosion of colour.

The hand of the photographer's assistant holding the flash has not yet lowered before Mrs Claiborne dashes across the room to adjust the lay of Elouise's dress and the flowers around it. She moves on to primping Elouise's ringlets of curls. "I don't think one frame will be enough. No, it won't do. George, I think we should take another. What do you think? One more?"

A tear escapes Mrs Claiborne's narrowly crunched eyes and falls on to Elouise's reddened cheek. It leaves a white streak through her rouge, the sight of which causes Mrs Claiborne to instantaneously freeze from her activities. Claiborne cups her shoulders, his hands large enough to almost meet across her chest, "Come mother. It's done. There nothing more we can do."

Elouise's glassy eyes cast loosely in the direction of the photographer who has just come up from under the black hood and begins to pack up the kit. The assistant, of adolescent years, lifts Elouise's arm to remove the prop from under it.

Mrs Claiborne shrieks from across the room, "Don't you dare touch her."

Claiborne grabs his wife even tighter and gestures for the young man to continue with his duties. The photographer joins his assistant and removes the prop from behind Elouise's head and back, then gently lowers her until she is fully reclined onto the seat of the chaise. With his index and forefingers, he closes her eyelids, ending her blank gaze. The assistant picks up her feet and extends them straight across the seat. This act causes the white flowers around the hem of her dress to tumble to the ground. The photographer crosses Elouise's arms over her chest, while his assistant makes the sign of the Holy Cross. Bowing politely, they both exit the parlour.

Claiborne is unable to console his sobbing wife partly because he sobs too.

※

The brass bell above the servants' entrance rings. Mrs Farraige places her glass of whiskey next to the almost empty bottle. It's a struggle for her to get out of her seat.

Unable to locate a figure through the frosted glass, she opens the door to find a rough and dirty looking boy holding a package wrapped in decorative coloured striped paper and bound with a bright red ribbon. His eyes immediately cast upon the black armband, which is so tight it appears to be cutting off the circulation from Mrs Farraige's upper arm.

"Parcel for Miss Waters mam." He thrusts the package upon Mrs Farraige before scampering back up the staircase and disappearing into the foggy morning.

Mrs Farraige takes a hearty swig at what's left in her glass, all the while staring at the package before her. She slams the empty glass down and pulls the ribbon open and then the paper, revealing the book within, *The Pied Piper of Hamlin* by Robert Browning Jr. She flips the cover open to find an inscription:

My Dear Miss Waters,

What a delight to have you in London. I shall hold you to your promise and insist that you join me for dinner. Until then, I thought you might delight in a little story about the powers of a childminder.

I can hardly wait to hear more of your adventures abroad.

Yours truly,

RB

Mrs Farraige pours what left of the bottle into her empty glass

Memento Mori

Bright green leaves, smooth and shiny, spring out from blackened tree branches. Branches that were once charred by the sunless winter sky. But today, their leaves sing to the 10,000 kelvin clear blue sky.

Below, family and friends of the Claibornes file out of St. James' Church in Sussex Gardens. Its steeple casts a long shadow in the morning light. So dark is the shadow that the mourners, cloaked in black, disappear when they step into it.

Other mourners gather along the wall of the church where their saints, cast in stained glass, gaze down on them but they do not look to their saints. Instead, they watch Elouise's coffin load onto a carriage. Much like the mourners, the black horses drawing the carriage are adorned in black feathered headdresses. The carriage resembles a glass box with gilded corners. Inside, purple velvet curtains frame Elouise's coffin.

A Funeral Director leads the procession, followed by the carriage, then clergy, then family, with friends and well-wishers making up the rear.

In the procession, Christian walks behind the Claibornes with baby Ash in her arms. Georgie sweats under the weight of his mother, who he props up by cupping his arm around her. Claiborne looks not to the coffin but up at the blue sky – a raven soars overhead.

Prof Brooks holds the hands of his girls, one on either side of him. Though the morning has taken a toll on little Rosie and he lifts her dragging feet from the ground and carries her slumped over his shoulder.

Christian looks back frequently at the newly wedded Mr and Mrs Woods. In the former Miss Lock's arms, another bouncing baby boy with a head of red curls and eyes of the striking shade of peridot green. They look familiar. Very familiar. Christian looks to the Woods, their light blue eyes and flaxen hair. Rosie's eyes are closed as she slumbers on her father's shoulder but Christian sees them anyway, they are the same shade of green and the same strawberry blond curls. She cannot see Prof Brooks' eyes either but she doesn't have to. For now, Christian is content to stare at his ginger tinted curls, which have escaped from under his hat.

Mrs Woods catches one of Christian's stealing glances and greets her with a friendly smile. Just beyond that warm smile, Mrs Farraige leers on.

It's not until Christian turns the corner to Craven Hill with Ash's pram and the two girls in tow, that McGhee lets up from a lamp post. Christian spots him, "Is that you Mr McGhee?"

"It is Miss Waters"

"Say hello girls."

Lily Bell and Rosie look on mystified at the man in tattered finery. His top hat frayed, overcoat patched and missing a few of the brass buttons, his oversized trousers belted at his thin waist and speckled with mud, while his unlaced boots are caked in mud, "How do you do, sir?

McGhee tilts his hat revealing a bushel of steel grey hair, "How do you do, girls?"

"Lilly Bell take Rosie into the kitchen and sit with Mrs Farraige. I'll be there shortly."

As instructed, Lily Bell rings the bell to the subterranean servants' entrance. Mrs Farraige answers, wiping her hands on the apron strung around her ample waist. "What are you two doing out here?"

"We're to wait for Miss Waters in the kitchen."

Mrs Farraige's eyes widen at the sight of McGhee as he hands Christian a note, "You girls go and have a seat at my table, I'll be just a second." The girls file in but Mrs Farraige lingers with the door ajar, training her ear to the curbside conversation.

From between his fingerless gloves, McGhee hands Christian a folded piece of paper. "From Mr Saline."

Christian rubs her forefinger over one of the corners feeling the ridges of its spun linen texture. She begins to open it but stops and looks up to McGhee. He looks on, void of any expression or emotion.

"Thank you for couriering my note Mr McGhee."

"You're more than welcome."

"Did you travel far?"

"Me a come from Ludgate Hill."

Unable to place Ludgate Hill, Christian's only response is a slightly confused expression.

"Fleet Street."

Christian is still befuddled and shakes her head.

"Not too far from St Paul's Cathedral"

"Ah, ok."

"Nearly a two hour walk."

"Oh my, you must be in excellent health.

He chuckles, "Not again. Mi legs not as strong these days. Mi used to travel the same distance in an hour but that was long ago."

Christian, "My dear sir, you must let me compensate you for your trouble." She reaches for her purse.

"It all right, miss. It all right."

Christian removes a coin and hands it to him. "Please, I insist."

McGhee pushes the coin back into Christian's palm and closes her fingers until they are wrapped into a fist, "Please miss, won't you read me this letter instead. It's about mi kinfolk back in Jamaica. Miss Waithman, mi friend, does occasionally read to me but let me trouble you today." McGhee removes a frail yellowed envelope from his inner coat pocket.

"Of course."

Christian slowly and carefully pulls the delicate paper from the envelope and opens it. It's so worn that little diamond shaped holes have formed in its folds. Christian takes a deep breath in anticipation of the task ahead but stops short when interrupted.

"Wait... from the beginning." McGhee points to the address on the envelope, "From the beginning, please."

Seaman Charles McGhee
His Majesty's Royal Navy
Cabin 4, Lincoln House
Portsmouth Naval Base

Christian looks up to find McGhee's silver curls fading to black. The sun beams brightly on his strong straight back. A gust of wind catches the hemp white, saltwater stained sail as it flaps violently in his face. The toes on his bare feet grip the jib arm as he inches closer to the mast. He climbs further up the mast until he reaches the crow's nest. He pulls himself through the narrow opening until he is able to stand on the wooden planks in the narrow basket. He looks below, at the sailors busy with chores, their voices slowly fading. McGhee smiles and lets out a deep sigh from within the bellows of his soul. His blousy hemp white shirt and black neckerchief blow freely in the wind as he looks out onto the horizon. Wherever his eyes fall, he is surrounded by every shade of blue. With the mast supporting his back he raises his right foot to the rim of the basket. McGhee removes a small telescope from the pocket of his breeches, which are just a shade or two darker than his shirt and cut to mid-calf. He extends the barrel of the telescope and brings it to his eye. Still nothing but blue.

2 February 1832

Dear Seaman McGhee

It is with our deepest regrets that we write to inform you that your wife, Sarah McGhee, and son, Saint Francis McGhee, are both deceased having fallen victim to the bloody revolt December of the year past. It has been reported that your mother, Mrs Mary McGhee, claimed their earthly remains and laid them to rest on the outpost of Shiloah in the parish of St. Elizabeth."

We are sorry for your loss.

With gratitude for your service to His Majesty's Royal Naval Fleet.

Lt General
Lord Admiral Stevenson
Port Royal, Jamaica

"Yes, yes, that's it. Thank you kindly miss. It's sorrowful news, mi know but mi need it. Mi need to hear it, like you need air. Yes, thank you indeed. I'll be on my way now."

"Mr McGhee, would you ... I mean can I get you anything to eat or drink before your journey back."

"There's no need young miss. Mi just fine now. You take care, you hear." Looking beyond Christian to the white terraced house behind her. "You're not to let these devils bring you down."

Mrs Farraige hastily steps back in and accidentally closes the door harder than intended. Christian whips her head around at the sound of it. When she looks back to McGhee, he is already hobbling down the street humming to himself.

Christian takes another look at the linen envelope simply addressed, "To Miss Waters" but in beautiful swirly lettering, before wedging it inside Ash's pram and heading into the house marked number 7.

Claiborne lays slouched over his desk. His shirt crumpled and unbuttoned. White stubble covers his jaw and neck, piercing his ruddy skin like a hedgehog. His empty whiskey decanter and glass stand guard over a pool of drool trickling from his mouth. A knock at the door jolts him to an upright position, "Yes."

Mrs Farraige enters, wringing her hands, "Sir, I'm sorry to bother you at a time like this. I know you're hurting but I can keep silent no more...sir. And Mrs Claiborne, well she's not fit to talk to anybody just yet. Poor soul. So, it's only right that I come to you. You see..."

"Yes, yes, let's have it Mrs Farraige. What's on your mind?" As he wipes the corner of his mouth with his shirt sleeve.

"Well, it's Miss Waters sir. There's something that ain't right about that girl. She's up to something. I know it. I just know it."

"Oh really, what exactly is it that you think she's up to."

"She means to harm this family, sir. She always so shifty, I hear moving up and down the stairs at night. Why, just the night before Miss Ella passed, I think she was in my kitchen concocting something devious. She was sent this book called The Pied Piper, you know the one about stealing children. Now, just today a vagrant looking negro passed her something, I think it was a letter. And they were out there whispering and conspiring. Just look around, she's only been here a few months and we're all..."

"We?"

"I mean..."

"Look Mrs Farraige, I hope you're not insinuating that Miss Waters had something to do with Ella's death."

Mrs Farraige steels her back and ceases wringing her hands, "That's exactly what I'm insinuating...sir."

"ReGodDamDicuLus! How dare you?"

"Please sir, allow me to introduce my brother DCI Craig of the metropolitan police."

DCI Craig enters the study and stands beside his sister, who is almost the same height as he and just as stout. He places his business card on Claiborne's desk, "Good evening to you sir."

"What is the meaning of this... this intrusion... in the sanctity of my own home."

"Please sir, will you not just hear me out. My sister has informed me that just the night before Mrs Brooks' passing, Miss Waters was skulking around her kitchen. The very next morning, Lizzy, eh, Mrs Farraige finds a poison berry on the same kitchen floor. Now, I would like to take a formal statement from Miss Waters. It's in everyone's best interest to get to the bottom of this."

On the other side of the door to Claiborne's study, Victoria rushes away carrying a tray with a sandwich and an apple.

The setting sun streaks through the window of the drawing room and onto the back of Christian as she wipes clean sums from the blackboard.

The amber coloured light shines through the frizz of her hair creating a halo around her face. The board is completely clean but she wipes on and on.

Victoria busts through the door to the drawing room, despite her explosive entrance she tiptoes over to Christian. Her racing heart causes her breath to blow her own wisps of blonde hair around in the sunlight. She struggles to keep her voice down, "Please Christian, come quick."

"Why, what's happened?" Despite Victoria's panicked arrival, Christian remains cool and calm.

"It's Mrs Farraige. She's got her brother round and he's a copper with the Metropolitan Police."

"And?"

"She's saying you've done in poor Mrs Brooks. That you've poisoned her with them berries."

"I see."

Victoria slings the tray on a nearby table and dashes to the door but does a double take when she turns to find Christian is still at the blackboard. "What...what are you doing?"

"There's nothing for me to do Victoria."

Victoria knits her brow and cocks her head to the side, "Go and tell 'em that you had nothing to do with it. That you ain't no murderer."

"I'll be doing no such thing."

No longer whispering, "Do you want to see yourself hanged? They wouldn't think twice of hanging a darkie, I've seen it before you know."

"Believe me Victoria, you needn't work hard to convince me of that."

"Well, go and speak up for yourself then!"

"I owe no one an explanation, let alone the likes of Mrs Farraige. That would most likely serve as an admission of guilt more than anything else."

Victoria's eyes widen.

"That means I have nothing to worry about and neither do you...unless you think I'm capable of such an atrocity too?"

"N...no, no I don't."

"That's that then. My concern is for the welfare of the children at this time and not my own."

"As you wish Christian."

Victoria retrieves the tray but before exiting, takes a look over her shoulder at Christian who has returned to cleaning the already clean blackboard. Christian ushers Victoria on with a reassuring nod. However, Victoria has only the chance to advance a couple of steps beyond the threshold of the drawing room, when the door to Claiborne's study swings open.

"Get out and don't you ever step foot in my house again."

"Now sir, I know you're grief stricken but you have to listen to reason."

"Reason! Are you mad? You listen to me and listen to me good. Get the hell out of my house now or I'll have your badge. You've no license to conduct an inquiry of any kind in my home. You are speaking of my family."

"No one is above the law, sir. The days of gentlemen like yourself having your way are over."

Claiborne grabs DCI Craig with one hand and opens the front door with the other. The DCI tumbles down the stairs narrowly escaping his head bashing onto the pavement below.

"You have no cause to return. Good day to you sir."

After slamming the door shut, Claiborne turns his attention to Mrs Farraige.

"You've crossed the line Mrs Farraige. How dare you think you could intervene in my personal affairs. The audacity!"

"Begging your pardon sir but I am only trying to look out for your welfare and that of your grandchildren. Can you not see what's happening under your very nose? First the dog, then your daughter... who will be next I wonder?"

"That'll be you Mrs Farraige. Gather your possessions and be gone from these premises with immediate effect. Leave a forwarding address with Miss Tarn and a month's wages will be sent to you."

"Consider it done. I'm glad to be rid of this place. But you mark my words Mr Claiborne, you'll rue the day!"

On her way back to the servants' staircase, she passes Victoria, "What do you think you're looking at. Back to work with ya."

Mrs Farraige hasn't the time to pass before Christian takes her place behind Victoria, smiling wryly.

"Oh, I wouldn't be so proud of yourself Miss Waters, you've yet to see the back of me."

"All the best to you Mrs Farraige," Christian swings the door shut.

Leaves on tall green stems sway away in the breeze. The stems are so large they eclipse the white cross bearing the name "Puddles".

Even though the half moon is covered by an occasional smokey grey cloud floating by, there's still enough light to illuminate the sky.

"Why are you here, Ogechi?" Claiborne approaches Christian in the garden.

She does not turn around to greet him. Christian's gaze remains fixed on the single light source as the clouds continue to sail over it.

"Why? Are you no longer glad I came? Is this no longer my home?"

"No, no not all. It's just that you're so close and yet remain so distant from me. I just can't fathom what you are thinking... thinking of me."

Silence.

Claiborne turns to leave but stops in his tracks at the sound of Christian's voice.

"One day, I will return to my home where my mother lies buried...somewhere... in an unmarked grave." Christian turns only her head in her father's direction, leaving one side of her face lit by the moon and the other cast in darkness.

"Are pretty flowers growing over her earthly remains? Answer me that and I'll tell you why I'm here."

"That Farraige woman is gone from this house Chi Chi, what more can do?"

Christian returns to the moon and speaks softly, "Answer me that and you'll know why I'm here."

"What's to be done, father."

"First, we'll have to discuss this with your mother."

"Do you think she's strong enough to handle this."

"Definitely not but what choice do we have."

Georgie sits across from Claiborne in his study.

"Can this really be happening?"

"Life has dealt us blows before but this... this is something I could never have predicted. My girl, my poor little girl."

Claiborne rubs his chest as his face grimaces.

"Steady on old boy. Everything all right?"

"Yes, yes. I suspect it's just a case of heartburn and only after one meal from Miss Tarn. She's no cook, that's for certain. Fair enough, I suppose, since we've not the means to pay for a proper cook. So, Farraige's absence might just serve us well."

"How will we manage?"

"It will take time but we'll have to adjust to Miss Tarn's culinary skills, of which she's greatly lacking. Though, I imagine she will improve in due course. Frankly, she's nowhere to go but up."

George looks on blankly, "I meant financially."

"So did I. Listen, I've been thinking of the girls. I think it's best we send the children to Brooks' parents in Sussex for now. A change of scenery might do them good, as will the country air. It will also ease Miss Tarn's workload until everything is sorted."

"And Miss Waters?"

"She will remain with us for as long as she likes... I mean since the children will only be gone for a short period, they will be looking for her upon their return. They've been through enough and deserve to be with someone they're comfortable with."

"Agreed."

"This isn't over Georgie boy. I feel it in my bones. Something ill is afoot."

"I'm inclined to agree on this point too, father."

"Over my dead body," screams Mrs Claiborne over the untouched bowl of soup on the four-legged silver tray on her bed.

"There's no point in upsetting yourself, Ivy. My mind is made up and my decision irreversible."

"What makes you think this is about your mind and your blasted decision."

"He's right mother, she had to go. Father has made provisions for a rather generous severance package. More than she deserves, I'd say. Especially when one considers the circumstance surrounding her dismissal."

"What circumstance was so dire that necessitated we let go of Mrs Farraige?"

"Save your strength, Ivy. I need you to pull through this and right now these tablets might be doing you more harm than good. Besides, I haven't the strength to relive all that's occurred these past few days. Can you not see we're *all* hurting?"

"These tablets are the only way I can sleep now, George."

Claiborne picks up the green bottle on her bedside table, "I know my dear, just mind how you go."

"But how will we manage? Our staff is already beyond skeletal and nobody knows how to stretch a penny like Farraige. You know how the Irish are with their thriftiness. We were lucky to have found her in London. There's all sorts scoundrels out there. And we've the girls to think of too."

Georgie looks to his father.

"About that, Ivy. I've also decided to send the children to the county with their grandparents - their other grandparents."

"What! How dare you make that decision without me."

"Look, they simply need to get out of this house for a while. It's been too much for them. Let them feel the fresh air and sun in Sussex. Leave the sorrow behind for a while."

"No. No. No. I simply won't hear of it. They need *me* right now."

"Mother, if you're right, you should appreciate the brief respite while you gather your strength. You're no help to anyone right now."

"And what of that blasted woman. We are all spinning out of control, while she stands in the centre of our undoing. Cold. Unaffected. Unscathed."

"She will remain Ivy. The girls will only be gone until... you are back on your feet and then we shall need a governess again. You can't deny that they're fond of her."

"We need a damn cook. Not some uppity negress walking around smugly judging us."

Claiborne exhales deeply.

"I want to know why?

"Why what?"

"You know exactly what I'm talking about. Out with it George. What devilish scheme is behind the dismissal of Farraige."

Claiborne clutches his chest, "Not now Ivy, I haven't the strength."

"Find the strength, George."

"Mother, allow me to speak on this matter. Mrs Farraige's brother is a member of the newly formed detective services of Scotland Yard. It seems as though she arrived at the bizarre conclusion that Miss Waters poisoned Ella and acting on her own volition, reported this falsehood to her brother."

"Oh my Lord. Oh my heavenly Lord. I knew it. I knew that wretch was up to something."

"Ivy, I'll not tolerate these false accusations. Not to mention the audacity to bring the police into it. As if there is any credence to this malarkey."

"But what if she's right. What if that, that ...woman poisoned our daughter."

"For what purpose. Why would Miss Waters do such a thing? You can't go around casting allegations willy nilly with neither proof nor motive. That's slanderous. Why, I could just as easily say the same of Farraige. What if her cooking poisoned our daughter. And you said it yourself, how nice it was that Farraige was making Ash's bottle. Think about it Ivy, Ella was ill long before Chi Chi showed up"

"Chi Chi? Who the hell is Chi Chi?"

"Enough Ivy, you know what I'm trying to say. I told you, I haven't the strength."

"Be reasonable mother."

"Why should I reason with you anymore. Nothing makes sense to me. How is it my daughter is gone and I'm still here. There is no greater pain than knowing you will never see your child again."

"Yes, Ivy. I know that pain too. She was my daughter too."

"Remove this tray from my sight."

"Mother you haven't eaten in days. Please do try..."

It takes major effort but Mrs Claiborne manages to rise from her sick bed and to her feet.

"You both are clearly under a spell cast by that black witch but I am not. I will go to the police myself and demand an inquest!"

Christian sits cross-legged on the oriental rug in the parlour. She reads out loud the story of young King Arthur. How he lived as a knave unaware he was the son of a king and of the latent powers within him. How his true identity remained unknown until he pulled his father's sword from a stone.

Rosie rests her head on Christian's thigh as she strokes Ash's cheek, who is sleeping soundly in the hammock formed by Christian's skirt in the centre of her legs. Lily Bell is tucked under Christian's wing. From her vantage point, she is able to read along with Christian.

"I don't want to go to nanny Brooks, I want to stay here with you."

"Me too. I want to stay with you Miss Waters."

"It'll only be for a short while. This will all be over with soon enough."

They read on about the triumphs, trials, and tribulations of the great King Arthur.

Mrs Claiborne hands a small white envelope to the same scruffy little boy who brought the copy of *The Pied Piper of Hamelin* intended for Christian, "Now you wait for a response. Understand?"

"Yes, Miss."

She hands him a coin, "Twopence, now and you'll get another upon your return. Understand?"

"Yes, Miss!"

His bony legs take off as fast as they can carry him.

※

Dearest Miss Waters,

I humbly ask for your audience on the fine evening of Thursday 14th June, nine o'clock, on platform 1 of Paddington Station.

Yours faithfully,

Jean-Luc Saline

Christian rolls the fine parchment into a slender tube and holds it over the opening of her oil lamp. It takes a few seconds but eventually the flame latches on. She playfully passes it back and forth, toying with it before the paper fully alights, then lays it to rest in her fireplace until it is nothing more than charred flakes.

She loops the black ribbon of her bonnet around her fingers as she fastens it to her head. With it, she allows one side of her lips to curl up into a half smile.

The door to Mrs Farraige's room is ajar. Christian gently pushes it increasing the opening by only a few more inches but it's enough to see inside the empty room. A bare mattress, a bed frame, and a tiny table chair are all that remains. Christian takes in a deep breath and lets out a silent chuckle.

She floats along the corridor and down the stairs taking her to the kitchen, where she gently closes the servant's entrance behind her.

※

Hurriedly and purposefully she makes her way along Craven Hill towards Praed Street. Before crossing Gloucester Terrace Christian sees the scruffy little boy on the paid errand for Mrs Claiborne running towards her. So focused on his destination is he, that he runs off the curb on Gloucester Terrace and into the path of a barrelling stagecoach. Christian pulls him back from what would have been certain obliteration. The horse and carriage pass so close, the fringe of his hair flutters in the downdraft. The two souls share a short yet loving look before he scampers away towards Craven Hill.

Scanning the fellow pedestrians at Paddington Station, Christian spots him almost immediately. She stops sharply. He has seen her too - the cinnamon coloured man. Their eyes fix firmly on each other. Everyone else fades into a blur of grey shadows but he remains in full focus. The blue of his suit stands apart from the darkness surrounding them, his eyes shine clear and beckon a passage to him. She takes a few more steps but stops again. Her heart pounds so hard it is almost visible through her blouse. It is he, who moves towards her. His friend begins the journey with him but is stopped with a hand to his chest.

However, there is no need for him to walk any further because he levitates to her. A bright orange and purple bird of paradise with spikey petals resembling a crown is extended to Christian. She grips the long thick stem but hasn't the time to marvel the flower, for her feet have left the ground too. They whirl around each other faster and faster, higher and higher. Until he reaches out to her, tenderly cradling her chin, bringing her closer to him. As their lips touch, their feet gently land on the ground.

"I am Jean-Luc Saline."

"I am Christian Waters... but family called, I mean call me, Ogechi... sometimes Chi Chi."

Saline kneels before her and kisses her right forehand.

"Nice to meet you, Ogechi. This is my brother Bernard St Côtes."

"Nice to meet you, Bernard." He bows before her and kisses her hand too.

Saline bends his arm, much like a handle on a teacup, and Christian pushes her arm through the passage made for her. They move on westward.

Mrs Claiborne swings the front door open to find the panting child before her, "Well, out with it."

"He said yes miss. He said eleven o'clock miss."

She places another two pence coin into his dirty little hand and closes the door without uttering another word. The boy is too bedazzled by the shiny coin in his hand to realise the slight.

※

The ink blue night sky bears witness to an unseen eye in the form of a black disc framed with a white nimbus. The stars wait turn to dance around it.

Saline holds Christian hand as they walk down the narrow towpath of London's Venice. He points to the colourless orb in the sky, "Tonight, we have a new moon. This is a good thing. A very good thing. It marks the beginning of the lunar cycle."

Christian looks to the sky, "But there's a storm in the light behind it. Surely that's an ominous sign."

"Is it? Storms are dangerous, yes. They're destructive, true. At the very least, they are disruptive. But, they can also be agents of change. Isn't that just what we need – the destruction of a corrupt system? Change? The start of a new cycle."

Christian doesn't respond but searches Saline's face for whimsey only to find none. This brings a little smile to her face.

Unbridled horses shake their manes and snort in their paddocks, as the three walk along the canal. Not far from the paddock, barge workers, who look and sound like the gypsies off Westbourne Grove, enjoy a game of cards on an overturned barrel. Their oil lamp casting a warm glow over their blackened faces. Both groups tip their hats in acknowledgement of each other.

Saline continues in Patois, "It was said that my grandfather came from a warrior people in Senegal. He was all but broken by the French in Haiti but when the revolution began he was reborn anew. He fought alongside the great Toussaint L'Ouverture. He owed the General everything, including his life and more important his liberty. It is in my grandfather's footsteps that my aspirations lay. Though he is gone from this world, I still call on him for strength, for insight, for direction.... for everything. Of course, I too have the distinct privilege of a link to General L'Ouverture."

"How? You're way too young to have known him."

"This is true but *his* grandson walks behind us."

Christian turns to Bernard. He smiles broadly and nods his head in recognition as he continues in Patois, "Yes, my grandfather had many children and they too had children. I am but one of many."

Christian stops walking and curtsies to Bernard, "I'm honoured."

Saline heartily slaps Bernard's back, "No man could ask for a better brother. I am indebted. Our grandfathers live on not only in spirit but also in flesh. We are continuing in their quest for freedom. For we will not rest until we are all liberated and what is rightfully ours is taken back.

Bernard, "And justice served."

The two men bring their fists together and look on surprised yet pleased when Christian puts her fist forward. She proceeds in her adoptive mother-tongue, "To liberty and justice."

Sing-along-songs waft out of the open windows of a tavern. The punters who are not singing are engaged in merriment so great their hearty laughter infects Christian. She chuckles as she looks on.

Barely audible beyond the raucous tavern is the sound of drums coming from one of the barges. Bernard lets out a caw-like call and the drumming stops instantly. Seconds later the door to the cabin slides open. A dark skinned Indian man emerges. His hair, awash with oil, is so black it is blue and falls beyond his waist. A full set of white teeth are unveiled between his handlebar moustache and chest length beard as he smiles at the sight of Bernard's approach.

"Mon frère!"

Bernard responds, "My brother."

The two men embrace but the Indian man is distracted by Christian who is standing just behind Saline, the hem of her black skirt and white petticoat gently blowing in the breeze. Saline leans in for his hug but is pushed aside when the Indian man bypasses him for an introduction to Christian.

"And who do we have here?"

"This is Ogechi."

"Ogechi?"

"Nice to meet you..." Christian pauses for the man to introduce himself but he remains silent, his jaw hanging low until Bernard manually lifts it back up for him.

"This is our dear friend, our brother, Sukhbir."

Sukhbir finally regains his composure and manners, "Won't you please come in."

He takes Christian's hand as she descends onto the deck. Saline jumps down from the deck and escorts Christian the rest of the way into the cabin.

Sukhbir steals the opportunity to silently mouth "What!" behind their backs to Bernard, who responds with a shrug, throwing his hands into the air.

The interior of the barge is painted dark red, made redder yet by lit oil lamps. Two women sit by a window. One African looking woman sits cross-legged on the floor between the legs of an Indian woman. She is braiding the African woman's hair. While the African woman is dressed in a standard hoop dress, the Indian woman wears a brilliant periwinkle blue tunic and pantaloons made from the finest of silks, adorned with an elaborate gold brocade. The centre part of her hair, each of her fingers, her neck, her wrists, her arms, her ankles – are all adorned with brilliant gold jewelry that glitters in the glow of the oil lamps and tinkles with her every move.

"Please allow me to introduce you to my sister Indranni and Bernard's sister Marianne."

The women greet Christian, "Hello, welcome. Please have a seat, make yourself at home." Christian takes a seat on a cushioned bench opposite the two women.

Marianne asks, "We have some dahl and it's still warm. Would you like some?"

"Em... dahl?"

Sukhbir chimes in, "It's curried lentils. Why not try a little? Anybody else? I've enough for everyone."

"Yes, thank you, Sukhbir. Very kind."

While Sukhbir ladles out the dahl, the women look Christian up and down. Marianne breaks the awkward silence, "How is it that you've come to know Bernard and Jean-Luc?"

"We met at an abolitionist meeting."

Sukhbir hands out cups of tea in round clay coloured cups without handles.

Saline takes a seat next to Christian, "It was the plight of a lost handkerchief that brought us together." He doesn't take his eyes off her as they sip on the tea. Meanwhile, everyone else's eyes flicker across the room at each other.

Christian looks up to find the skirting glances, "This is delicious Sukhbir, I've never had tea quite like it before."

"Ah, this is spiced tea from the northern region of India, Punjab. Where I'm from. It's mixed with a little anise seed."

"It's delicious."

"I'm glad you like it."

Sukhbir follows up with two small wooden trays, one for Christian and one for Saline carrying their meals. Saline leads the way by tearing off a corner of the roti and uses it to scoop up some dahl. "Like this." He gently places the morsel on Christian's awaiting tongue as she quivers in anticipation.

So transfixed by the fledgling couple is Sukhbir, that Bernard has to nudge him to get his attention so that he can hand him his tray. Sukhbir uses the opportunity to question the vision before him by raising his eyebrows. Bernard still has no answers, he only shakes his head with a half-smile.

Sukhbir takes a seat on a cushion on the floor next to Marianne, whose hair is now freshly braided, "So what do you think Ogechi? Any good?"

"It's delicious, I've never had anything quite like it before."

Sukhbir quips, "Thank you."

Indranni throws a comb at Sukhbir.

Marianne explains, "Sukhbir would love to take the credit but it was Indranni who made the dahl." She leans in and kisses Sukhbir tenderly on lips.

This act momentarily stuns Christian and she grapples to recover, "Oh thank you Indranni."

"My pleasure. I'm happy to show you how to make it. It really is quite easy.

"I would love that."

The newly made friends gab away, as Christian explains where she is from. In the midst of their conversation, Sukhbir pulls out a carved wooden box depicting an elaborately decorated elephant.

"Ogechi, have you ever smoked ganja before."

"No, I've never smoked anything before."

Marianne, "Quakers, they don't smoke and drink, is that right?"

"Yes, you're quite right but I wouldn't describe myself as a Quaker, though I respect their principles."

"How would you describe yourself?" Sukhbir asks.

"In some ways, I *am* a daughter of a Quaker but in other ways, I am not. I suppose you could say that I'm in a transitional phase. In many respects, I'm just learning of my true identity and it is giving me cause to think about who I once thought I was and what I might become."

Though Sukhbir is carefully listening to Christian he removes a long pipe adorned with ivory carvings from a silk case. "Life is a series steps Ogechi. It is a wise person who stops to question who they are before moving on."

Christian nods her head, "Yes, one step at a time, someone else just reminded me of that fact."

"Well, consider ganja and aid in your journey. It might just give you flight."

The jingling of her jewellery punctuate Indranni's nod in agreement.

Sukhbir addresses Bernard and Saline, "Let's cast off chaps".

Bernard unties the barge from the towpath. Saline then uses a long pole to push off and out into the water enabling Sukhbir to pilot to the little round islet of Regent's Canal.

Once back inside, Sukhbir breaks up the buds and the leaves and stuffs the mossy looking substance into the pipe. After igniting the base, he sucks furiously on the nib of the pipe until white vapours pour out and curl around his moustache. Sukhbir inhales and holds the fumes in his lungs before passing it to Christian. She tries to do the same but breaks out into a violent cough before the first puff has the chance to hit the back of her throat.

Saline takes the pipe from her. "Like this." He takes a monstrously large inhalation then hands the pipe to Marianne. Christian follows the pipe around the room and tries to hide the disappointment in her eyes. So preoccupied with the pipe is she, that she doesn't see Saline reaching to place his hand on the nape of her neck. She turns to face him as he leans in and places his lips over hers, parting them open. He proceeds to pump the smoke from his lungs into her lungs. She inhales as much as she can before opening her eyes to find him smiling at her. "Hold it for as long as you can." Christian nods. The others cheer her on as the pipe is passed. About thirty seconds later, she gently exhales the smoke and giggles girlishly at her actions.

Sukhbir pulls out three drums and the men remove their shirts. They place the drums between their legs and pound out a tribute to their ancestors. To their brethren in bondage. To their future. To the night.

Christian and Marianne remove their skirts and in their corseted waists and join Indranni on the bow under the moonless sky and dance for their sistren. For their dreams. For their lives.

On the towpath, an elder Englishman in top hat and long coat stops with his dog by his side of the canal. He looks on blankly at the spectacle before him. He removes his pipe and gives it a little sniff before continuing on.

Soil piles up around a granite headstone. Two carved angels look down on the words:

> *Here lay the earthly remains of*
> *Elouise Georgina Brooks*
> *Beloved Daughter, Wife & Mother*
> *Born 1827 - Died 1855*
> *May she live on in our hearts forever*

A shovel bangs into a hard surface and stops. Two non-cherub looking men kneel over the coffin and brush the remaining soil away with their hands. They look up to Mrs Claiborne who is standing at the foot of Elouise's grave. "Are you sure about this madam?" says one of the men. "This might be a bit grim for a lady such as yourself," says the other.

"Open the blasted thing. We haven't all night!" barks Mrs Claiborne.

The two men exchange a nervous glance before one of them climbs out of the grave. He picks up a crowbar and hands it to his colleague, who places his feet on either side of the lower half of the coffin. Before opening the coffin, they share another nervous glance. He applies the crowbar to the locks and levies his weight by placing the leg up along the side of the grave and pulls with all his might. It takes but a few seconds to pry the lid of the upper half of the coffin open, busting the wood around the lock free.

Mrs Claiborne leans in and then staggers back. She collapses down to her knees, her black hoop skirt melts around her. The man who is already out of the grave rushes to her aid. At first, she waves him away but quickly changes her mind, "No wait. Go and get this man for me." She hands him the card of DCI Craig.

Pre-dawn mist wraps around the bollard as Sukhbir, sporting a pinstripe suit and crowned by a turban, moors the barge. Bernard is still inside engaged in a passionate kiss with Indranni. Each time he says goodbye to her, she pulls him back for another kiss. Saline stretches as he emerges from the cabin.

While Christian is bidding her farewell to Marianne, Sukhbir uses the stolen moment to finally talk to Saline, "I've never seen you so... happy!" Sukhbir's eyes remain firmly on Christian as he speaks but Saline remains speechless and just stands grinning.

Sukhbir gives up on his friend and instead focuses on Christian, "Ogechi, I'm reaching to find the words that would express my pleasure for having made your acquaintance. I hope to see you again very soon."

"Yes, I would like that too. Thank you for your hospitality. I shall remember this evening always."

Christian turns and waves farewell to her new found friends. Sukhbir and Marianne lock arms as they wave back, "See you soon Ogechi."

Bernard slaps Saline on the back and the three make their way back down the towpath.

Christian waves goodbye to Saline and Bernard in front of number 7 Craven Hill Gardens and remains to watch them walk away into the misty morn. She holds the bird of paradise close to her chest.

Just before entering the black iron gate, something on the roof catches Christian's attention. It's a raven. As soon as the bird is spotted it takes flight, disappearing through the cloud that's come down to the earthly plane. Christian motions as though she was about to follow the bird but aborts the mission before it begins. Under the raven's flight path she notices the faint outline of a horse and carriage down the road. She takes a few steps towards it but stops again. Instead, with a shake of her head, returns to the house but not before taking another good long hard look at the carriage.

After making her way through the empty kitchen, she has only the opportunity to take a few steps up the narrow servants' staircase before the door at the top of the landing swings open. Light floods in. Claiborne staggers on to the landing blurry eyed. One of the corners of his collar has broken free and juts away from his shirt. His hair is more disheveled than usual. His suspenders hang freely about his waist causing his trousers to slouch under his pot belly.

He smiles nervously at Christian, "There's no need for you to worry Ch... Miss Waters.

"Two more men attempt to squeeze into the tiny space on the landing; one is DCI Craig and the other in the uniform of a Metropolitan Police Officer. DCI Craig motions to speak but is silenced by Claiborne's raised hand, "Miss Waters, these men...Police Officers would like you to accompany them to The Old Bailey."

"Why?"

"They seem to be labouring under the impression that you are somehow responsible for Ella's death."

"And if I choose not to go?"

DCI Craig struggles to step in front of Claiborne, "Thank you Mr Claiborne but that'll be all for now. Miss Christian Waters, I am arresting you on suspicion for the murder of Mrs Elouise Brooks."

"I see. Well, I cannot come upstairs and be arrested until you've exited the landing."

The three men awkwardly try to clear the exit but instead bumble into each other as they decide who should go first.

Christian finds Victoria in tears when she enters the hall on the ground floor. She rushes to Christians side with a brown paper package but is blocked by the arm of the uniformed officer.

Claiborne interjects, "Steady on."

Victoria pleads to Claiborne, "It's just a cheese sandwich, sir."

DCI Craig takes the package from Victoria and opens it. All eyes are on him when his shoulders drop to find bread and cheese. He recovers by standing straight and signaling with a nod to the uniformed officer, who in turn removes a set of handcuffs from his belt and proceeds to lock them around Christian's wrists.

Claiborne protests, "I say, is that completely necessary?"

"Yes Mr. Claiborne, it is."

The bird of paradise falls to the floor as she is being cuffed. The uniformed officer takes Christian by her elbow and is about to lead her out of the house, when Georgie makes a mad dash down the stairs, tying his dressing gown shut in the process. He halts the procession by getting in front of Christian, "Don't say anything Miss Waters... Christian. We'll be there shortly to represent you and this farce will be over soon enough."

Christian nods her head in agreeance, "Thank you, Georgie."

He leans in and kisses her forehead.

DCI Craig grabs her other elbow, relieving the uniformed officer, "Fetch Black Maria."

"Yes, sir."

The uniform officer signals for the waiting carriage to pull up to number 7.

Claiborne and Georgie are on the heels of DCI Craig, "We're right here Miss Waters. We're right behind you." The carriage is little more than a black locked box with small slits for windows. "Don't you worry about a thing." The uniformed officer unlocks the back door and pulls his prisoner in. "We'll be there as soon as we can." Christian's handcuffs are linked and locked to a rail above her head. "There's no need to worry." The door is locked shut.

The carriage pulls away leaving Claiborne exposed to his prying neighbours, who have gathered in their night clothes in their doorways. He waves his arms furiously at them, "Away with ya." Until he stops to clutch his chest in agonising pain.

Georgie helps him back into the house where Victoria closes the door behind them with Christian's bird of paradise in hand.

Xaymaca: The Land of Wood and Water

Darkness sweeps across the horizon of Xaymaca. The sunless landscape, void of its hues of green, turns black. Grey clouds envelop its mountain range and all who reside there. Gusts of wind carry the whispers of workers from field to field and up into the canopied mountaintops, then back down into fields.

Christian is swaddled to her mother's back as she walks down the road leading from the Claiborne Plantation. Like the rest of Jamaica, the sky over them is an ominous mix of dark blue and grey. Palm trees sway violently back and forth threatening to break in the wind.

The pending storm stirs up dust around Emuesiri's bare feet and whips around her ankles. From over her shoulder, Christian watches her mother pump water into a wooden bucket. Just beyond the pump, a man emerges from the cane field. The soiled rags on his body are unable to absorb the sweat streaming from every ridge on his body. Though the light is dim, his black skin shines brilliantly aided by his glistening perspiration. He smiles at Christian peering out over her mother's shoulder as he extends his hand to Emuesiri. He almost retracts it when he hears galloping horses approaching but she grabs his hand firmly. Moreover, it is their eyes that lock indefinitely.

The horses stop behind her but she does not turn to address them. Instead, she places a tin cup containing water in the man's blistered palm.

One of the men shout out from atop his horse, "Oi, what's this? What you doing out 'ere?"

Emuesiri snaps back, "Can you not see the man is desperate for water!"

The same man dismounts his horse and removes a whip from a strap on the saddle, "Who do you think you're talking to girl?" He slings his whip over his shoulder as he approaches. "This water ain't for niggers."

When she turns to face him, he stops dead in his tracks. The scar stretching from the corner of his eye down to his cheek reddens like it did the night Claiborne gave it to him. It twitches uncontrollably, as he fights to rid his face of fear, "Get on with it and back to work with ya."

The man in rags slowly raises the cup to his lips and swallows, then passes the empty vessel back to Emuesiri. She guides his hand under the nozzle and pumps twice, which is enough to re-fill the tin cup. All the while she smiles at him.

One of the men on horseback grows impatient, "What the hell is going on down there?"

The man with the reddened scar flares his nostrils, "Shut it Nance."

He drains the second cup down to the last drop and gives Emuesiri a slight nod as he hands it back to her. Their eyes lock once more, just for a millisecond, before he submerges himself back into the cane field. She returns the tin cup to the hook beside the pump.

As soon as it placed on the hook, it is knocked off, "No man can drink from this now."

With all his might, the scarred man stomps on the vessel but it does not break, nor even bend. He stomps again… and again, and again. His colleagues laugh at the spectacle. Even Emuesiri affords herself a slight curl of the mouth before she picks up the bucket and continues on her way. The man screams at the sight of the perfectly intact cup and picks it up, swinging it into the cane field. He watches Emuesiri float along the road and screams again. He mounts his horse and tries to charge into the cane field at the same entry point as the man in rags but his horse rears up as it refuses to cooperate bucking him out of the saddle. His body hits the ground with a mighty thud sending hurls of dust around him. He screams again sending his friends into further fits of laughter.

Torturous screams bellow through the cane field but the man in rags does not alter his course. His heart races as fast as his feet, while the cane's sharp leaves slice away at his flesh. He comes to stop at a shallow brook. By levying a rock and clawing away at the hard red soil, he creates a little burrow. He opens his mouth and extends his tongue. On it, a black cast iron key. He places the key in the hole and covers it, first with the soil and then with the stone.

Emuesiri picks up a blue and white painted china plate with nothing more than clean chicken bones on it. She is about to walk away when a soiled napkin is tossed on to the plate, covering the design of a finely painted windmill and its accompanying wheat filed. She walks past a portrait of Claiborne, who is standing proudly next to Mrs Claiborne. His hand gripping her chair where she is posed with a back so firm and upright it does not come close to touching the back of her chair. Her dress is an array of pink and white lace, as is that of the infant girl in blond ringlets seated on her lap. Beside Mrs Claiborne, a young boy with dark wavy hair watches Emuesiri, as she makes her way to the kitchen.

Claiborne adds water from a pitcher to his glass of rum occupying the vacant space left by his absent plate. He swirls the etched glass causing the slice of lime to act on behalf of a spoon, mixing the two elements until they become a homogenised tonic. He brings the glass to his mouth and takes a hearty gulp.

Emuesiri returns to the dining room and stands before the family portrait as she clears the rum bottle and pitcher from the table. "Leave it." Emuesiri lowers her head in observance of his wishes, then turns to leave. "No, wait." Claiborne catches her wrist and pulls her close. He looks up and into her eyes as he encircles her waist. He presses his ear into her womb. He presses harder and harder until the side of his head is almost buried into the pleats of her skirt. He takes in a deep long breath. Rising from his chair he pulls her closer to him. Claiborne kisses Emuesiri as though he were drinking her - sucking her in from the inside out. He runs his hands over her breasts, lingering over her nipples. This excites him, encouraging him to kiss her again as he pulls her hills of green coloured blouse, from her skirt and unbuttons it.

He manages the first few buttons when he is interrupted by screams of a woman coming from the courtyard. And then there is silence. He unbuttons two more when a crashing sound comes from the back of the house. This time he pulls away from Emuesiri and heads towards the kitchen. He finds the cook, Misty, a brown skinned woman in her late sixties, trembling in the corner holding young Christian. More screams come from beyond the back door, this time it is clear they are screams of men. Claiborne reaches for the latch to the back door, when the Misty pleas, "I beg you sir, don't go out there."

He looks at her puzzled but before he has the opportunity to respond, footsteps are heard above him pummelling through the wooden floors of his house. Misty faintly whimpers, "Oh no." She looks down at the puddle of urine under her skirt.

"Stay here Misty and watch Chi Chi...Lock the door behind me."

Claiborne rushes to the door leading back to the dining room but it swings open before him. He hasn't the time to react, as he is bashed in the face with the butt of an axe knocking him to the floor. The black man from the water pump emerges through the door, the rags are gone from his torso and he stands bare chested over Claiborne. He raises his axe up - blood already dripping from it. Claiborne raises his arm over his head in preparation of the pending strike.

The axe is about to come down when a resounding scream of "Nooooo." reverberates throughout the kitchen. Emuesiri, stands by the side of the man and grabs the handle. "No. Tie him up." Another man pushes by her and upon her command, rolls Claiborne over and hogties him as she buttons her blouse.

The last thing Claiborne sees is Christian crying and reaching for him before a sack is thrown over his head. He tries to comfort her, "Shhh, shhh it's alright baby. Shhhh, shhhh." Emuesiri retrieves Christian from Misty's clutch.

Thunder breaks from the beckoning clouds, drowning out the cries of agony from around the house, the fields, the valleys, and mountains. Lightning blasts through the sky illuminating the full scale of blood and bodies on the ground, if only for fleeting seconds. Panicked horses break free from their tethers and flee the bedlam.

Emuesiri leans into the sack covering Claiborne's head and whispers in his ear, "You'll stay safe if you follow my instructions. Do not come after me. Leave here and go back to where you come from. Never come back." Claiborne's head remains motionless. She tries again, "Do you understand me!"

"Why are you doing this Katherine?"

With Christian still on her hip, "Misty stay with him. Make sure no harm comes to him tell them this one belongs to Emuesiri."

Four more men, barefoot and dressed in rags, charge into the kitchen, they are fully loaded with rifles and other forms of artillery. The bare chested man takes one of the rifles, "Emuesiri it's time to go."

By standing Christian on the table, Emuesiri swaddles her to her back with her apron. She then tucks one of the pistols into the waist of her skirt.

The bare chested man calls for the men to leave. Emuesiri files out with them and does not look back but Christian does, "Da Da."

Claiborne calls for them through his bloodied mouth and hooded face, "Ogechi! Katherine! Don't do this Katherine. Katherine! Stay with me, my love." He struggles violently to free himself from the binding but to no avail. The kitchen door is slammed shut and locked.

Black iron bars swing open to her cell but Christian maintains her focus on the view outside her window. The sun is about to begin its long descent into tomorrow. She lays on a bench made of bricks and mortar, painted white many years prior. For a pillow, she rests the back her head on her folded arms.

"Miss Waters?"

"Ces't moi."

"Miss Waters, you're to be remanded to the interview room."

With another look out the window, Christian lets out a deep sigh as she rises from her perch.

Mud and blood splash onto the hem of Christians long black skirt and white petticoat as she walks down the rutty road leading to the Claiborne Plantation. She runs her hands through the bushy weeds growing on the side of the footpath. Clouds in the moonless night sky rain on her, while utter chaos reigns around her. She walks on.

Two men in rags knock down a man in a hemp coloured shirt and breeches. They take turns in bashing the downed man's head with a rock. As one of them comes up, a shot rings out piercing his back. He drops instantly. Christian walks on by them unnoticed. His comrade doesn't need to retaliate, as the owner of the shot is dragged from his horse by a group of women all dressed in rags. The horse breaks free of its reins and jumps over the fence leading to a fallow field. One of the women, her braids twisted around her head like a crown, picks up the dropped rifle and pulls the trigger aiming at the fallen man. It clicks but there's no fire. She doesn't hesitate to use the butt of the rifle to smash the man's head. Despite her gallant effort, her blows are ineffective and the fallen man writhes about in pain on the ground. The rifle is taken from her by the only man in the group. He completes the job in two blows.

The newly freed horse gallops by Christian. She speeds up to keep pace with the horse. Faster and faster, until her feet leave the ground.

Rain and blood and soil merge, it gushes out from every orifice on the land. This thick dark red union is still running over Christian's feet when she stops at a bulletin board at the end of a hall in the Old Bailey. A wanted poster depicting two men at large for the bombing and robbery at the Bank of England is pinned front and centre of the bulletin board. They are clearly black men. She looks back and forth between the two men and then focuses on the widow's peak and almond shaped eyes of one of the men before quickly looking away ensuring her discerning gaze is not captured by the uniformed police officer, who is close on her heels.

A shiny black metal door adjacent to the bulletin board opens. Christian steps into the room to find Claiborne seated next to Georgie on one side of a long table, while DCI Craig, Dr Moss, and a well-dressed balding man, Lord Banks, sits along the opposing side. In front of each of the men, a pile of neatly stacked papers. But it is the man seated at the head of the table, that causes Christian's eyes to linger. It is the familiar face of the Right Honourable Sir Arthur Riverton who she instantly recognises as the elder statesman from the abolitionists' meeting, causing her to smile ever so slightly to herself.

"Preposterous!" Claiborne rises from his chair, "Pure and utter nonsense."

Georgie gently pats his father's forearm, "Steady on old boy," encouraging him to return to his seat. It works, Claiborne lands in his chair with a thud.

Dr Moss continues with his remarks, "Mr Claiborne, will please be reminded that I am bound by two oaths; one, to speak only the truth at this deposition and two, by the Hippocratic Oath, which mandates that as a medically trained doctor I practice my trade to the highest degree of impartiality. To this, I add that the conclusion drawn from the autopsy was shared with my esteemed colleagues from the Royal College of Physicians, all of whom agree with my findings. So before Mr Claiborne asserts that my report is ... nonsense ... I would like to remind him of whom he is addressing."

Georgie interjects, "Your Honour, my father does not purport to possess the same level of medical knowledge as the - esteemed - Dr Moss but he is in a position to speak on behalf of Miss Waters' character, begging the validity of the charge of murder alleged against her."

"Your Honour, I, along with other attending physicians at the mortuary, do hereby swear that Mrs Brooks died of acute arsenic poisoning. As evidenced by the nature of her rigor mortis, which was well developed at the time of exhumation. Post-mortem lividity was purplish-red and fixed. Conjunctival congestion was present bilaterally. Whitish viscid mucoid secretions were present around mouth and nostrils. All consistent with arsenic poisoning. This is medical evidence, my dear sirs, and will not falter. If I am removed from this case, there are many more qualified physicians waiting in the wing to replace me with the exact same findings. For my result is not emotionally derived or subject to personal opinion but is based soundly in scientific fact."

"Your Honour, while we are certainly interested in soliciting a second opinion regarding Mrs Brooks...my sister's death, I would like to remind Dr Moss that he was treating her for a long standing illness well before Miss Waters even arrived in the country. I aim to prove that my sister's death was a result of misdiagnoses in life, so as you can imagine I have little or no regard for Dr Moss' findings in her death. We foremost maintain that Miss Waters is in no way responsible for my sister's demise and without any proof of the said allegations, we motion to dismiss the charge against her. The damage that Dr Moss' incompetence has rendered, has to be not only challenged but reigned in before he destroys another life."

DCI Craig spins a paper around so that Georgie can read it, "Master Claiborne, you seem to be deluded. Dare I say bewitched." He trains his glare to Christian, "As you will see, the evidence against Miss Waters is quite credible and substantial. We have proof that not long before Mrs Brooks' passing, Miss Waters prepared a concoction of sorts and did give it to Mrs Brooks to drink. Here, is an affidavit prepared by Mrs Farraige, the Claiborne's cook for the past eight months, since their relocation to Bayswater. It details the dubious comings and goings of the accused. Also, I present a page torn from a book indicating a recipe calling for the use of wild berries and plants, which can only be described as a poisonous elixir."

Georgie responds, "Yes, DCI Craig we've all read the complaint and I maintain Mrs Farraige's allegations are without merit and fail to provide any evidence of Miss Waters' having knowingly and willfully poisoned my sister by way of arsenic, as Dr Moss claims."

The Right Honourable Riverton takes a deep sigh and removes his tiny round steel rimmed spectacles, "Miss Waters, the crimes alleged here are of the most serious nature and carry a sentence of death by hanging. I've heard from the prosecution and your counsel. Before I determine whether a crime has been committed and to carry forward to trial, I would like to hear from you, which is why I have requested your presence."

Lord Banks finally speaks, "I object your honour. As the lead prosecutor for the Crown, it is most irregular to hear from a ...prisoner and I cannot permit this act."

"Agreed, but since Miss Waters has not yet been formally charged, she is not officially a ward of the state and therefore not a prisoner. Miss Waters, what say ye?"

"I am innocent of these allegations brought against me."

Lord Banks, "What of this torn page Miss Waters. Do you deny this was found in your possession? Do you deny that you made the concoction outlined in this...this recipe and administered it to the deceased?"

"You do not have to answer him," cautions Georgie.

"I do not deny this sir. I did, in fact, administer the formula derived from this recipe to Mrs Brooks... and to baby Ash." Gasps echo out of the tiled room from the three men seated on the opposing side of the table.

"Please Miss Waters, as your counsel, I advise you not to take this course of action any further."

Christian ignores Georgie's waiver, "When I first met Mrs Brooks I suspected that she might be suffering from arsenic poisoning; excessive sweating, nausea, hair loss, sallow complexion, these are all common and well documented symptoms. However, I did not act sooner because I believed her to be receiving treatment from a medically trained doctor, which I am not. Not yet, at least. I've had some medical studies but I am far from completing my education. Since Mrs Brooks was under the expert medical care of Dr Moss, I second guessed myself and focused on my duties as Governess to Lily Bell and Rosie. But when I saw the sores covering Mrs Brooks and Ash, I immediately knew what her doctor did not..." Christian casts a discerning eye to Dr. Moss, "...that not only was she contaminated with arsenic but so was Ash. There wasn't much time at hand, so I went to the Portland Library with the expressed desire to find a book that might offer a cure with ingredients I could source locally. Fortunately, there I found the answer in a book called *King's Poisons and Cure Alls* but the library decided that I wasn't fit to check the book out, so I tore the page out. It shouldn't take much effort to match the torn page to the book."

Lord Banks asks, "If what you say is true, why conduct yourself in such a surreptitious manner. Why not make your actions clear to everyone around you?"

"My secrecy was determined by forces beyond my control. By those like Mrs Farraige who sought to discredit me at every turn. When I saw that Ash was not taking to the breast, I knew that not only was contamination present but time was of the essence. I couldn't afford to have my actions blocked by those who lacked trust of my intent, so I made haste. I am, however, sorry." Christians turns to face Georgie. "I'm sorry for not acting sooner. I quietened what I knew to be true in favour of our good doctor here, instead of raising the alarm. Consequently, I was only able to save Ash."

DCI Craig snarls, "You lie! How do you explain them voodoo dolls then ..."?

"Voodoo dolls? Do you mean the rag dolls I made for Lily Bell and Rosie? They love those dolls and practically made them themselves."

"And The Pied Piper that was secretly delivered to you?"

"What are you talking about? I know nothing of this secret delivery of The Pied Piper."

"Go ahead Miss Waters. Try to deny this." DCI Craig slides a copy of the slim book across the table. "Whatchya planning on doing with them kiddies, eh?"

"That book does not belong to me. I've never set eyes on it before."

Georgie thumbs through pages and discovers the inscription from Browning to Christian. He reads it aloud, "

Dear Miss Waters,

What a delight to have you in London. I shall hold you to your promise and insist that you join me for dinner. Until then, I thought you might delight in a little story about the powers of a childminder.

I can hardly wait to hear more of your adventures abroad.

Yours truly,

RB

"This must have come from a dear friend, Mr Browning. I heard he was an author but am unfamiliar with his work, so he promised to send something of his to read. But I never received this book. Mrs Farraige must have intercepted and withheld my correspondence."

Like a dog with a bone, DCI Craig continues, "You're evading my question Miss Waters."

The Right Honourable Riverton interjects, "That's quite enough DCI Cr..."

But DCI Craig ignores the warning, "Tell the truth Miss Waters, you mean to harm this family. Don't ya. Planning on snatching them little kiddies, eh?"

Claiborne rises from his seat, his nostrils a flare, "How dare you." He slams his fist down so hard, the spectacles of the Right Honourable

Riverton bounce up from the impact. "I've had just about enough of this farce."

The Right Honourable Riverton tries to regain control of the proceedings, "Will everyone please calm down or you will all be reprimanded, as I see fit." He turns to Claiborne, "Mr Claiborne, I and I alone, will determine when this inquest is over. And as for you DCI Craig, I hope you're not suggesting that the great Robert Browning is conspiring to kidnap the Brooks' children, are you? Because if you are, you better have proof or I'll see that charges of slander are brought against you. So there will be no further claims of voodoo or kidnapping without adequate evidence. Do I make myself clear?"

Lord Banks turns to Claiborne, "Good sir, may you be reminded that it was your wife that requested this inquest, which led us here today. And to be mindful that we are only performing our civic duty and will not fall subject to your disdain for doing so."

"My wife is grieving for her child, thus explaining her lapse in judgement. What, good sir, is your excuse for persecuting this poor young girl? My family, my home and all who dwell in it are exclusively my concern."

DCI Craig, "Not if a crime has been committed, Mr Claiborne. There was a time, not too long ago, where your sort could get away with murder but not anymore. It's a new day. The Metropolitan Police are well within their purview to execute investigations into murder wherever they may fall. Including your home...sir. "

"I see. So, this charade has naught to do with impartiality and justice. It's a vendetta. DCI Craig, do you seek to enact some revenge upon me because I have and you have not? Are you out to punish my sort? Or, is this some measure of retribution for me terminating your sister's employment? Well, let me remind you – all of you – you're all public servants. Salaried from my taxes, so that you can serve me, not persecute me. You haven't the right to this intrusion and it will not be tolerated – I assure you. Now this quack, who calls himself a doctor, could have saved my little girl. Instead, Ella has paid for his recklessness and incompetence with her life and almost that of her baby. It would seem as though he is not content to stop there, he as the audacity to cover it up by casting blame elsewhere. Well, I will not stand idly by and have a member of my family... or of my staff denigrated, berated and then falsely accused of a crime punishable by death to cover your negligence. I'll see you ruined. All of you."

"That'll do Mr. Claiborne. The prosecution has failed to provide any evidence of foul play, let alone murder. Unless that changes, I motion this inquest be brought to a halt. Furthermore, I motion that a new inquest be opened to investigate charges of gross negligence and medical misconduct against Dr Moss. DCI Craig, you will in no way engage any further in this matter. I will assign a new investigatory team to this case. Miss Waters, unless any evidence is presented to suggest otherwise, you are free to go on your own recognisance. And on behalf of the Crown, I offer my sincere apologies for this grueling ordeal." The Honorable Riverton hands her the slim book on the table, "I do believe this is your property."

The setting sun hits Christian's cheeks upon her exit of the Old Bailey, lighting the gold flecks in her skin and cause her eyelids to lower to half-mast. With the sun in her eyes, she is only able to see the outline of a figure approaching her. It is not until McGhee stands directly in front of her, blocking out the sun she is able to discern who it is. He embraces her, "I see by your expression it is good news." He takes the opportunity to press a folded paper into her palm and whispers, "From Mr Saline." At that very second, Georgie greets McGhee.

The horse's hooves clop along the cobbled road. The carriage squeaks and rattles over every rut and bump. Snatches of conversations from pedestrians fade in and out as the three occupants of the carriage sit in silence. Claiborne places his hand over Christian's, who sits beside him. When Georgie catches sight of the tenderness of his touch, Claiborne changes course and removes his hand. Instead, he opts for a reassuring tap on the back of her hand.

Christian remains motionless. Instead, her gaze is firmly fixed on the view of the Thames fading in and out of the buildings on the Strand. Georgie is firmly fixed on the opposing window, at the merchants and market dwellers bartering their wares.

As Claiborne settles the carriage fare, Georgie uses the opportunity to search Christians face. She doesn't back away from his gaze. They stare long and hard into each other's eyes. Claiborne is only just done completing the transaction when Victoria bursts through the front door breaking the trance between Christian and Georgie.

"Mr Claiborne! Come quick sir! It's Mrs Claiborne."

"What is it now Miss Tarn?"

"She not waking up. I think she's taken too many of them sleeping tablets."

Terror registers over Claiborne's face as he attempts to run towards Victoria. However, in a matter of a few giant steps, Georgie is first through the front door. Claiborne attempts the same manoeuvre but his old bones restrict his effort to hasten his step. Behind him, Christian calmly strolls up the stairs and closes the great black oak door behind them all.

※

A myriad of musical notes glide across The Round Pond in front of Kensington Palace. Brilliant white swans bob up and down on the water as though they are dancing at a grand ball. The violinist doesn't take his eyes off the waltzing birds as he works feverishly to provide them with music. He seems completely unaware of the woman dressed head to toe in black seated on a bench the other side of the pond.

Saline takes a seat on the other end of the bench from Christian. She smiles once she realises who her neighbour is and motions to slide across but her actions are halted once he speaks, "Stay where you are. Face forward and keep your eyes forward."

Christian reluctantly complies, as she scrunches her eyebrows.

Saline continues, "I've much to explain but there isn't the time, so I'm afraid I must keep our visit brief."

"I understand."

"No. I don't think you do."

"I do. I do understand. This is about the stolen gold, isn't it?"

Now it is Saline's turn to scrunch his eyebrows, "Yes. How do you know?"

"I recognised you from a wanted poster in the Old Bailey."

"Ah, I see. Are you all right?"

"I am."

"I'm leaving Ogechi. We can stay in London no longer. The circle of safety around us grows smaller with each day and the cloak of anonymity more transparent. We should have left a long time ago but we stayed... I stayed for you. I thought that I would somehow corrupt you by exposing you to our enterprise but seeing as how you were just charged with murder, I thought perhaps, you might be a little more... accepting?"

The two share sheepish smile through a stolen glance.

"Oh,... I was not charged with murder."

"That's interesting because not being charged is not quite the same as being innocent, n'est pas?"

Christian affords him one more sly half smile.

"And you? Are you a bank robber?"

"Guilty as charged. I'm guilty of stealing what was stolen from our people. Though, what we took is just a mere drop in the ocean when compared to what was taken from us. From what we are due."

Mounted royal guards gallop past Kensington Palace raising dust and disrupting the tranquility of the locale. Saline looks yonder to a wooded area, where Bernard lays back on a tree, his hat pulled down almost obscuring his face and an open book before him, though his eyes watch those of the soldiers riding past him.

"Sukhbir can only fence the gold outside of England. We will then have the resources we need to further our mission. It is imperative that we leave for Paris on the morning of the eleventh of July. Come with us."

Christian turns to face Saline and finds that he is already facing her.

He continues, "Come with me. I will love you and care for you to the end of our days."

Christian returns her gaze to swans who dance no more because the music has stopped. Instead, the fiddler stands with the violin lowered to one side of his body and the bow on the other. He no longer watches the giant white birds but instead watches the two figures in black clothing on the bench, "Saline, it's time to go."

Saline rises to his feet, "Stay where you are. We leave from Dover on the eight o'clock ferry." And with that, disappears from her side.

Christian is careful to keep her eyes on the pond, though she watches the man who has not yet returned to playing his instrument. She waits a moment or two to alter her gaze to the tree where Bernard lay but he too is gone. By the time she looks around, she is heading to the palace gates.

Christian rises from her seat and makes her way through the trees towards Bayswater.

Early morning light beams through the purple petals on the foxgloves growing over Puddles' grave. The flowers are the only signs of life in the garden. With intense scrutiny, Christian watches them from her open window as she finishes braiding her hair. She is still watching the foxgloves when she buttons the top of her blouse but not before rolling the blue and yellow bead between her fingers.

Like a cat awakening from a nap, Mr Fen steps out of the shed and stretches. He catches a glimpse of Christian in her window, causing her to hastily step back out of sight. "Damn it," as she winces at her actions.

※

The burning in the back of Georgie's throat doesn't stop him from gulping down what appears to be Mrs Farraige's whiskey when Christian enters the kitchen carrying a wicker basket of groceries in the crook of her arm.

"I've news for you," Georgie rasps.

Instead, of addressing the oddity of Georgie sitting at the kitchen table and his drunken state, Christian places the heavy basket on the table and removes her bonnet before taking a seat next to him. For the first time since arriving in London, her nerves plague her as she wraps the black ribbon from her bonnet around her finger.

"Just this morning I met with Riverton. Though the second inquest has only just begun it has already been determined that Ella died from *accidental* arsenic poisoning. And that her death could have been prevented if detected in time - just as you said. It seems as though the shade of green, Scheele's green, so in fashion today, is highly toxic. More specifically, it contains arsenic. She passed it to Ash through her breast milk."

"Is that what was used to paint her parlour?"

"The very same. And dye her dresses. And god knows what else." He swats his arm across the table causing the glass and bottle to fly across the room shattering into a thousand pieces upon impact of the tiled wall. "Have you ever heard of anything so ridiculous? All, to look as though we are keeping abreast. In step with the finest."

Christian notices his trembling arm as it rests on the table wet with whiskey. She rests her hand on his forearm and instantly he stops trembling, "I'm so sorry Georgie. Truly I am but you mustn't blame yourself. How were you to know."

"But you knew. How? How did you know?"

"I didn't know either. Well, I wasn't sure. I suspected something was wrong but wasn't certain. It wasn't until I learned that my mother was gifted with the ability to heal, that I realised that I was obliged to act, regardless of the consequence. It was said that she came from a long line of healers and with that, had the ability to see beyond the physical plane.

She possessed a heightened sensitivity to people not only to their maladies but to their innermost thoughts."

"And from your father, you must have inherited your kindness."

Christian withdraws her hand.

"You saved Ash. Thank you. I shall never forget that."

"And I shall never forget that you saved me. Thank you Georgie." Christian wipes his tears, which have just started to fall.

※

The mid summer's sunset renders the sky in a rich indigo, punctuated with shades of magenta and mango. A gentle breeze ripples the hem of Christians skirt. The moon's emerging brilliance catches her tear streaked cheeks.

"Gardening at this hour?" Claiborne stands behind her as he notices the shorn foxgloves from Puddles' grave in her hand. Christian's grip around the stems is more like that of truncheon than of delicate blossoms.

"It's time for me to leave this place."

"This place is your home ... just as much as it is mine. I would very much like for you to stay."

The two stand in silence with eyes fixed on the speckled white orb in the sky.

"I've given a great deal of thought to your presence here and what it means to me. With your permission, I would like to reveal your true identity to Georgie. He should know. He deserves to know. Pretty soon, he will be all you have and vice versa."

Christian has not moved. Not her eyes, nor her mouth. Just her skirt in the breeze.

"My clock is ticking out, I feel as though it's about to strike midnight any minute now. Please Ogechi, see it in your heart to forgive me.

Please. You ought to know that I never stopped loving you or your mother but I hadn't any other option before me."

Christian turns to leave the garden.

"Ogechi wait. Please Ogechi, don't go."

"Thank you for helping me remember my mother but you ought to know, giving me away was the best decision you could have made for me. And for you. Goodbye father. You'll not see me again."

Georgie sits alone in the dining room. He looks at his pocket watch suspended from a gold chain and then to the golden face on the grandfather clock ticking away in the corner. He lets out a sigh from the depth of his frustration as he throws his napkin on to his untouched meal of scrambled eggs and toast.

The door to Claiborne's study slowly opens, "Father? Father?"

Slumped over his desk lays the mountain of the shell belonging to Claiborne. Before him a silver tray still bearing the remnants of his dinner - an empty plate, with the exception of a few crumbs, a soiled napkin, and a knife and fork. His empty glass, however, has rolled off the table and smashed onto the floor. The morning light peeking through the curtains shimmers on the splinters. Claiborne's mouth hangs slightly agape but his eyes are wide open as though he was straining to look at the painting of his long lost plantation in Jamaica.

A man places his leather medicine bag at his feet and rolls down his white sleeves, before removing his jacket from a hook in the entrance way. He places his hand on Georgie's shoulder, "My condolences Mr Claiborne. I understand you've sustained many a tragic loss as of late but you've got to bear up and be strong for your mother." The man looks back at Mrs Claiborne sitting at the bottom of the stairs in her nightgown, her body rocking back and forth, while her head jerks about aimlessly. She whispers incoherently to herself but occasionally blurts out equally incoherent declarations.

Georgie's eyes, however, are fixed on Christian's black bonnet on the hook where he left his bowler hat. The bonnet's ribbons hang freely and sway in the breeze caused by the men carrying the stretcher where Claiborne's body is wrapped from head to toe in a grey blanket.

Waiting by the horse drawn ambulance, DCI Craig removes his hat at the sight of Claiborne's earthly remains. Though not obvious, his smirk is certainly discernible.

The man notices Georgie's preoccupation with the bonnet, "So, she's gone, you say?"

"Yes. Sometime during the night."

"Do you know where?"

"No. She made no mention. Of course, she made no mention that she was leaving either."

"Well, I suppose she was spooked off," the man motions to DCI Craig. "I mean, he's quite literally circling the house like a vulture. In any event, your father's death was caused by a heart attack - plain and simple. His weak heart was long known. Quite frankly, I'm surprised it didn't happen sooner. The only way it could have been murder was if his heart attack was induced."

"Is such a thing even possible?"

"My dear boy. Anything is possible, the question here is, is it probable? And I say no. Not unless someone slipped digitalis into his supper."

"Digitalis?"

"Yes, it's a poison derived from a class of plants called nightshades. But this would have to have come from someone with a knowledge of botany and medicine."

Georgie finally turns to face the man.

"Be at ease Mr Claiborne, there are more cases of unsuccessful poisoning attempts via digitalis then successful."

From the window in Christian's room, Georgie looks down onto Puddles' grave, where bright green, freshly shorn stems poke up from the ground. Reflecting onto the pane of glass he sees Christian knelt, cutting the foxgloves from the garden.

A deep sigh quivers as it breaks free from his chest.

He takes a seat at her table where he notices an envelope propped up on the blossoming African violet addressed to him. He wastes no time in ripping it open. He pulls out a thin gold chain with a little blue bead decorated in a bright yellow design suspended from it.

Victoria sits at her table in what was once Mrs Farraige's room, reading *The Tale of the Pied Piper* aloud. A bee buzzes around a vase of bright purple foxgloves before her. She opens her window and lets it out. She smiles as she watches it fly off into the blue sky.

※

"So that's it?"

"I'm afraid so Mr Claiborne."

My father's estate is essentially bankrupt?"

"Essentially."

"And my mother's assets?"

"As you know, by law your mother's assets were your father's assets, which he assumed a long time ago. And yes, your mother's family estate in Weymouth was long ago dissolved."

"Yes, of course, I know but do you mean to say there's nothing left. Nothing?"

"Your townhouse in Bayswater is fully paid off, as are all of the furnishings, which I believe came from Weymouth. There is a small purse of £168, which should be enough to see through until you've completed the BVC. But that is it... The exception being the small parcel of land left from your family's liquidation of the Jamaican plantation near Ocho Rios, I believe. Not much, a little over an acre. But this was left solely and quite specifically to your sister."

"I see. I had no knowledge of this land. Can you arrange for the auction to take place in Jamaica? I wish to forward the proceeds to my sister's widower and children, who will certainly need the leg up."

"I'm sorry Mr Claiborne, this land was not intended for Elouise. It is intended for your living sister. Your half-sister, Ogechi Claiborne."

"Ogechi Claiborne? I know of no such person!"

"Oh. I beg your forgiveness for my candour. Last we spoke, your father and I, well he made his intentions expressly clear. He also said that he would inform you of his decision."

"Listen here. There appears to be some sort of mistake. I have no half-sister. I've never even heard of this person called Ogechi."

"Perhaps you know her by the name her adopted parents gave her, Christian Waters. I understand that she resided with you until just recently."

Masses of barristers, bankers, clerks, and journalists perform an artful dance across the busy intersections in the ancient City of London. Nowhere else, is the flock of men in black suits and hats thicker than at the junction of the Bank of England and The Royal Exchange, as they make their way home during the evening rush hour. Georgie, out of step and off balance, stumbles along eastward on to Cheapside in the direction of St Paul's Cathedral. The sun burns into his blue iris and he hasn't his bowler to hide under.

The shouts of a young boy dressed in dirty clothes and an even dirtier face are audible as he bellows the headlines of the evening edition of *The Guardian* but Georgie does pay attention to what he is saying until a copy of the paper is thrust into his face.

"Sweeper of Fleet Street Dies Leaving A Fortune"

Under the headline, a rendering of Charles McGhee in all his tattered finery with his broom in-hand standing in front of the obelisk on the foot of Ludgate Hill. Georgie snatches the paper from the boy and begins reading the article on the spot.

"Oi, that I'll be tuppence!"

Georgie searches the pocket of his waistcoat and tosses the boy a coin, which serves to pacify him.

He takes only a few steps more before employing the use of a wall to prop himself up. Although distressed, he keeps reading:

The affable Charles McGhee, known as the Sweeper of Fleet Street, passed away this morning. Apart from serving in Her Majesty's Royal Navy and being of Jamaican origins, little is known of Mr McGhee despite operating in the busy thoroughfare of Ludgate Hill and Fleet Street for the better part of 30 years.

Though he could be easily mistaken for indigent, due to his shabby appearance, it has now been brought to light that he leaves behind the vast sum of £700. The clerks of Lloyds Bank told how this black man dressed in rags came in at the end of every day without fail and deposited the pennies tossed to him over the course of 30 years. He often mentioned that he'd not a soul to spend it on. Why he did not lavish it on himself, we will never know

Instead, he bequeathed his fortune to Miss Waithman, daughter of the former Lord Mayor of the City London, The Honourable Robert Waithman. It is reported that she came to respect Mr McGhee, as he never failed to show up for his unofficial job of street sweeper. She was always mindful to send out a hot bowl of soup and bread and often clothed Mc Ghee in her late father's wardrobe.

He is reported to have conducted himself with dignity and took great pride in his work, even when those around him failed to see him in the same light.

Miss Waithman released a statement earlier today vowing to donate every penny of Mr McGhee's £700 fortune to the abolishment of slavery.

※

Red ambers glint through the night sky as Christian soars past the Arc de Triomphe. A little glow increases as she inhales. The breeze wafting off the black water below attempts to take Georgie's bowler hat from her but she catches it before liftoff. Behind her, Saline emerges from the evening's tenebrosity and wraps himself around her body. Her dark burgundy taffeta bustle skirt and matching jacket crunch in his embrace. She leans her head back onto his shoulder as wisps of her hair blow in his face tickling him, eliciting a smile. She holds the slim brown cigarette up for Saline to take a drag. More ambers fly off and then dissipate.

Indranni steps out of the cabin, warm shades of the red interior outline her figure, "Dinner's ready."

Bernard comes to the door behind her, "Yes but they're not."

Christian leans over the railing to get a better look at the waves hitting the bow of the vessel. The helm of the boat pierces through the dark waters and into the night.

It's all black.

References

The Black Jacobins

1. James, C.L.R. *The Black Jacobins: Toussaint L'Ouverture and the San Domingo Revolution*, London, Penguin, 1938

2. The Bank of England
    a. Contents of the BoE gold vault.
    b. Entrance to the vault via the sewer.

Mi Nuh Sen You Nuh Come

1. Jamaica's Cockpit Country is famed as the land settled by the Maroon's earning the colloquiums of The Land of Look Behind and Mi Nuh Sen You Nuh Come.

    a. Thompson, Kimone. "Where is Cockpit Country." *Jamaica Observer*, 21 May 2015
    b. Shoumatoff, Alex. "The Proud People of Jamaica's Untracked Cockpit Country." *The Washington Post*, 31 December 1978
    c. "Cockpit Country." Encyclopaedia Britannica

2. "Ackee." Wikipedia

3. "Craven Hill." Wikipedia

4. Samuel Birch. Wikipedia

Nightshade

1. Author and poet Robert Browning Jr was a frequent visitor of his artist friends, the Flower-Adams, residents of Craven Hill. His olive complexion raised speculations of ethnic origins in his day, leading many to believe that he was of either Jewish or southern European extraction. However, evidence suggests that he was most likely of Afro-Caribbean ancestry through his grandmother's lineage, Margaret Tittle. Browning's paternal

grandfather was a slave trader and profited from plantations in the Caribbean but his father was an abolitionist.

    a. Burns, Monique. "Two of the World's Greatest Lovers – Elizabeth Barrett and Robert Browning – Were Descendants of Blacks." *Ebony* May 1995: 97 – 150

    b. (Browning in Craven) Baker, T F T, Diane K Bolton, and Patricia E C Croot. "Paddington: Bayswater." *A History of the County of Middlesex: Volume 9, Hampstead, Paddington*. Ed. C R Elrington. London: Victoria County History, 1989. 204-212. *British History Online*. Web. 15 August 2018. http://www.british-history.ac.uk/vch/middx/vol9/pp204-212.

    c. (Browning in Craven) Browning, Elizabeth Barrett, and Browning, Robert. *The Romantic Letters of Elizabeth Barrett Browning and Robert Browning*. Musaicum Books 2017: 30

2. (Tyburn) Baker, T F T, Diane K Bolton, and Patricia E C Croot. "Paddington: Tyburnia." *A History of the County of Middlesex: Volume 9, Hampstead, Paddington*. Ed. C R Elrington. London: Victoria County History, 1989. 190-198. *British History Online*. Web. 15 August 2018. http://www.british-history.ac.uk/vch/middx/vol9/pp190-198.

3. Ira Aldridge. Wikipedia

4. Jack the Lad. Phrase Finder

5. Dick Turpin. Wikipedia

6. Joshua Glover. Wikipedia

7. Sherman Booth. Wikipedia

8. Fugitive Slave Act. Wikipedia

9. Johnson, Hall. "Aint Got Time To Die." Afrocentric Voices in Classical Music

Xaymaca: The Land of Wood and Water

1. Xaymaca translates to Land of Wood and Water, which is an Arawak/Taino idiomatic expression for a fertile land.
   a. Griffiths, Rhys. "Jamaica: From Slavery, Sugar and the Worst of Western Colonialism to Reggae and Rastafari." National Gallery, *History Today* 5 December 2017

2. Charles McGhee
   a. Jenkins, Terence. "The Lord Mayor's Daughter and the Crossing Sweeper." *London Tales*, Acorn Independent Press, 2012

3. The Baptist War
   a. "Case Study 4: Jamaica (1831) – The Rebellion." *The Abolition Project* 2009
   b. Further reading – National Library of Jamaica

Miscellaneous

Jamaican Patois Dictionary – Jamaican Patwuh

30394652R00082

Printed in Poland
by Amazon Fulfillment
Poland Sp. z o.o., Wrocław